WELCOME TO THE BIG CITY

Arnie heard the footsteps and felt the presence and then strong hands had a hold of his upper arms. Two men, one on each side. "Hey!" he yelped.

Neither man said anything. They didn't let go of him either. They turned him around and he saw there was a third man with them.

This guy was big. About as tall as Arnie and with wide, heavy shoulders. He wasn't fat, though, like Arnie's friend back inside the bar. This fellow wasn't the least little bit fat, no sir.

"Whyn't you just—" Arnie didn't have time to finish the sentence. The third man punched him in the stomach, hard, while the first two continued to hold his arms.

Arnie was taken by surprise. He would have braced himself if he'd known the blow was coming, and it wouldn't have hurt so awful bad. As it was, the big fellow's fist buried itself wrist-deep or thereabouts, and drove every scrap of breath clean out of Arnie's lungs.

Other *Leisure* books by Frank Roderus:
STILLWATER SMITH

Hayseed

FRANK RODERUS

LEISURE BOOKS   NEW YORK CITY

A LEISURE BOOK®

September 1998

Published by

Dorchester Publishing Co., Inc.
276 Fifth Avenue
New York, NY 10001

ISBN 0-8439-4432-3

Hayseed

"You!" the bouncer snapped when he came into the parlor. Arnie stood, waiting to ask what the problem was. Before he could open his mouth to form the question, James threw his first punch.

Arnie blocked it without taking time for conscious thought. The training Mr. Thomas had given to him came into play, and Arnie flicked the punch aside with a quick swipe of his left forearm. "Hey, listen, what've I—?"

James tried again, this time with a left. Arnie met it with his other forearm and deflected it wide. The blow would likely have taken his head off had it landed. But it did not.

"Listen, dammit, what is this?"

James threw a short, sharp underhand blow that was supposed to land in Arnie's belly and double him over. Arnie stepped quickly to his left, pulling James out of position. Arnie could have hurt the man then with a left hook to the kidney, but he still couldn't quite believe that a scrap was inevitable. If he could just get the man to *listen*. . . .

"Get him, James," Mrs. Baxter hissed from the other side of the room. "Hurt him before you throw him out. Hurt him bad."

It began to occur to Arnie that no one here was particularly interested in listening to anything that he wanted to say. His side of the story—whatever story this was—just wasn't welcome.

7

James spun to face him and, head bobbing and hands extended more like he wanted to wrestle than to box, began to stalk Arnie across the heavy, floral-print rug that softened the floor and deadened the sound of his footsteps so that all Arnie could hear at the moment—all he was listening to, anyway—was the muted whistle of James's heavy breathing as the bouncer tried to trap him in a corner.

That was almost funny, Arnie thought. Hell, Arnie'd spent practically his whole life sitting on top of good horses trained to cut calves out of herds and make the stubborn bovines go where they were wanted in spite of their own natural instincts. And putting a man into a corner and keeping him there was just another form of cutting cows, except probably easier. After all, folks weren't half as wild as those spooky old range cattle, and Arnie could handle them easy enough.

He could see two steps before James took them where the man wanted to go and how he expected to get there. Arnie let him think it was all working just as nice as you please. Then, about the time James thought he had himself a calf trapped tight into a corner, Arnie quit pretending and let James know that he wasn't facing some city boy here. Arnie feinted ducking to his left, stopped the motion, and stood tall while he hammered James's face with a hard, straight right.

Damn punch stung Arnie about as bad as it must have hurt James, and Arnie wondered if he could call a time-out so he could find his gloves and pull them on. Somehow he didn't much think James would go for that.

The bouncer blinked, but he didn't yet look like he realized there was anything different about this latest in his string of victims. He shook his head, spraying some blood that was beginning to stream out of a broken nose, and once again crouched as he bulled his way straight ahead.

Obviously the man expected Arnie to back away. Instead, Arnie moved close. Quickly. And sent a crushing blow into James's breadbasket. James turned pale and the wind was forced out of him in a great, wheezing whoosh.

While James was preoccupied with trying to regain his breath, Arnie stepped lightly to his left and tattooed the bouncer's eyebrows and forehead with a rapid-fire series of left jabs. The combination didn't do a hell of a lot of good for Arnie's knuckles, but it did have the desired result. James commenced bleeding from fresh cuts over his eyes as well as from his already busted nose.

If this kept up much longer, Arnie thought, the inside of this parlor was going to look more like an abattoir than a fine and fancy whorehouse.

James still hadn't quite caught up with the notion of what was going on here. And Arnie had no intention of letting him make any adjustments either, for, as powerful as the man looked to be, Arnie thought it best that he not find himself on the receiving end of too many of the punches that were flying between them.

James punched. Arnie weaved and bobbed and ducked.

James punched. Arnie flicked his wrists, deflecting James's fists, and responded with hard countering punches of his own.

James punched. Arnie danced lightly backward until James ducked his head and plodded forward, only to be met by sudden assaults that left his ears stinging and his eyes full of his own blood.

James punched and Arnie steeled himself to accept some damage to his own hands. He wanted to end this. Soon, before the bouncer tagged him with a lucky shot. He began concentrating on the shelf of the burly fellow's jaw, hoping to drop him and put him out of the game with a carefully placed right that he would throw with all his weight and leg strength behind it.

"Get him, you son of a bitch," the madam was screaming at her employee. "Don't let that kid do this to you."

James stopped still. He was in the center of the parlor, blood dripping off his chin and his elbows onto the rug. His head was hanging, and after that short flurry he looked exhausted, used up and worn out. It was obvious he wasn't accustomed to anyone standing up to him. He especially was not used to the idea that anyone who did stand up to him could do so with impunity, the punishment going James's way and not that of the unwelcome customer. James eyed Arnie like a played-out bull while with slow and deliberate care he reached into a back pocket for a soiled bandanna. He shook it out and then used its folds to clear the blood from his eyes.

"Can we talk about this?" Arnie asked. "Will you at least tell me what's wrong? Why you're doing this?"

James didn't answer him and neither did Mrs. Baxter. She was still much too busy shouting threats and curses to pay attention to anyone else. Arnie wasn't sure if her fury was directed more toward him or toward the ineffective bouncer who hadn't been able to beat up on what had looked like easy pickings. Not that he supposed it mattered overmuch.

James finished wiping his face, stood, and gulped deep for some air.

"Are you done, mister?"

James didn't answer. He looked at the blood-soaked kerchief, then shrugged and carefully folded it before returning it to his back pocket.

But this time, when his hand came forward again, Arnie could see the glint of steel in it.

The man had a knife. And he held it like he knew how to use the ugly, scary thing. He held it low, cutting edge upward and the butt of the haft nestled in his palm. Arnie knew absolutely nothing about knives or how to fight with them—that hadn't been any part of Mr. Thomas's course of instruction— but he knew enough to be scared half out of his wits by the sight of the deadly looking blade.

This fight was turning into something a hell of a lot more serious than anything he'd ever experienced before. This fight was not just for fun, not for bragging rights, not even for domination. This fight could be to the death if the bouncer and the screeching madam had their way.

Arnie backed away slowly, feeling behind him with his feet before committing his weight, eyes never leaving James. More accurately, with his eyes never leaving the slowly weaving point of James's knife. The blade had an almost hypnotic effect on Arnie. His mouth had gone dry, and his breath was coming short and shallow.

There was nowhere behind him to run. James stood between Arnie and the wide double doorway into the foyer. Mrs. Baxter and a dimly perceived bunch of female faces filled the smaller doorframe that led into the back of the house. Arnie was trapped, pure and simple. He figured he knew now what a calf felt like when it faced a good cutting horse. Except the fate of the calf wasn't likely to be half as bad as what James seemed to have planned for Arnie.

Lordy, Arnie thought, the single, silent word as much a prayer for delivery as it was an exclamation of despair.

He backed up hard against an end table beside the sofa where he'd sat earlier. James took a step toward him. Then another. The knife caught a shaft of bright lamplight and reflected it off the walls and the ceiling.

James came forward another step.

Arnie reached behind him, his hand fumbling for . . . something, anything, he didn't know what, didn't care. Anything.

The only thing on the table was the coal oil lamp, its hand-painted globe hot and bright, its base heavy with lightly scented oil.

If that was all there was then that would have to do, wouldn't it?

Arnie picked up the lamp. Threw the thing. If it started a fire . . . hell, if it started a fire, so what? This wasn't his place, and he didn't have any reason to care about Mrs. Baxter's future well-being, did he? Not when certain questions about Arnie's own future had yet to be determined.

He threw the lamp as hard as he could, straight at the knife in James's hand.

The brittle globe shattered, and the weight of the much heavier glass base knocked the knife from James's grasp. The flame blew out once the protection of the globe was gone, thank goodness, and what was left of the lamp scattered harmlessly over the rug. Nobody had better walk barefoot in there until the dang rug was taken out and thoroughly beaten. But then it would need some cleaning to get James's blood out of it anyway, wouldn't it?

"Kill him!" Mrs. Baxter shouted from the doorway. "Kill the SOB!"

James didn't so much as look to see where his knife had fallen. He reached behind him, on the other side this time, to dip into a different back pocket.

And this time what he produced was even scarier than the knife had been.

This time he had a pistol in his hand. A revolver. Small. A shiny, nickel-plated thing.

The weapon's small size did nothing to make it less awful.

Arnie looked into the muzzle of the little gun. It seemed to be aimed, he thought, pretty much at the bridge of his nose. He could see the dull gray tips of bullets at the front of the open chambers of the cylinder.

He could see James's broad, blood-smeared finger on the trigger.

He could see James's finger begin to move.

Oh God, Arnie thought. This was not the way things were supposed to've been.

Chapter One

"He who is afflicted with lust, if only within his own heart, is doomed to perdition. To everlasting agony. His nostrils will be filled with the stench of sulfur, and his flesh will be seared by the eternal flames of damnation. He who pursues the fleshly pleasures of this earth shall be *damned*."

Arnold Rasmussen stared at his knuckles. Hard. He carefully avoided raising his eyes. He did not want to meet Brother Spense's accusing glare. For surely Brother Spense's message, as it so often was, was directed solely . . . and exclusively . . . and with painful accuracy . . . at Arnold Rasmussen.

Arnold Rasmussen avoided looking at Brother Spense. But he did not, could not, long avoid glancing down the pew immediately in front of the Rasmussen pew to where the Mulraneys always sat. From Arnold's position beside his father he could see the nape of Katherine Mulraney's neck, so slim and soft—well, presumably soft; Arnie had no personal experience to draw upon when he arrived at that assumption—so downy and delicate, visible beneath the prim curls and starched bonnet that she always wore.

Arnie Rasmussen lusted after Katherine Mulraney. And the worst of it was that he was not at all as repentant as Brother Spense would have had him be had Brother Spense known of the lust—Arnie preferred to think of it as love—that resided deep within Arnold Rasmussen's young heart.

"Those who are given to earthly pursuits must perish in the

13

eternal fires of Hell," Brother Spense warned Arnie, the accusing voice from the pulpit booming out for all the Rasmussens' neighbors to hear. "But those who love decency and who choose to follow the Lord's path will be saved," Brother Spense proclaimed. "Those who choose to follow the Master will receive the salvation of everlasting life. Amen."

Brother Spense's amen was followed by a supporting chorus of amens from the congregation. Half a moment later, the choir broke into a closing hymn while Brother Spense and Elder Thomas hurried down the center aisle to take up positions there. When the song was finished, Brother Spense delivered a brief benediction and a reminder, "Don't forget our picnic dinner on the grounds, now. Those of you who forgot to bring food are welcome to stay anyway. There's plenty for everyone. Now God bless you, one and all."

A buzz of conversation filled the small church and the people began filing slowly toward the doorway, where Brother Spense and Elder Thomas waited to shake their hands and offer words of welcome, of encouragement, of brotherly love.

Arnie and his father remained in their pew, waiting for Arnold's mother to return her robe and emerge from the choir room so they could all leave together. Katherine and her family were already gone, Arnie noted. But that was all right. Surely the Mulraneys would be staying for the monthly picnic. Please God they would stay, Arnie breathed silently, then felt a pang of guilt because his prayer was directed by the lust that was within his heart.

Still and all . . . please God the Mulraneys would stay for the picnic.

There! He'd done it again. And he'd meant it.

He lifted himself on tiptoes and peered over the heads of the throng that crowded the center aisle. Yes, there was the back of Katherine's sweet head. He saw her there and his heart turned over in his chest and a tightness filled his throat.

God, she was beautiful. Buxom. Rosy-cheeked. Heartbreakingly pretty. She was everything Arnie yearned for, everything he wanted. Right there in the flesh.

Katherine was a big girl. Five foot six, perhaps, with light brown hair and large, laughing, light brown eyes. Full lips and

14

full figure. Her ankles—Arnie knew because he'd glimpsed them on more than one occasion—were slender and tidy. Her waist was small, at least in proportion to her bosom, and her hips broad and comely.

Practically anyone in Alder Creek, apart from a few men blinded by their own emotions, would have conceded that Katherine was the prettiest girl in Prairie County, likely the prettiest girl anywhere in Wyoming Territory.

Not everyone, however, would concede that Arnold Rasmussen was the lad most likely to win fair Katherine's heart.

Arnie himself understood, better in fact than anyone, his own unworthiness.

Arnie himself realized that beside the beauty of Katherine his awkward bulk was but so much unappealing meat.

At six foot three and with the approximate build and heft of a young ox, Arnie Rasmussen felt oafish and ugly. His coarse, slightly reddish hair was a perpetual tangle usually, and mercifully, hidden beneath the crown of a battered old Stetson that his father had discarded years ago. He had high cheekbones, pale blue-gray eyes, a nose twice broken by the frantic hoofs of soon to be branded calves, and a weather-beaten complexion that Arnie himself likened to that of aged suet.

Handsome he most definitely was not.

But in his heart, deep in the innermost recesses of his dreams, Arnie Rasmussen was convinced that he and he alone could worship Katherine Mulraney in all the ways, with all the depth of intensity that she truly deserved. He believed implicitly that of all the males on earth his adoration was the love most true and therefore the love to be most valued.

In this manner alone did Arnie believe himself worthy of his first and only true love.

As for Katherine . . . he sighed . . . today, finally, today he would approach her. Today he would hint to her of the gifts he had to offer.

Today Arnold Rasmussen would declare himself. Or if not actually declare then . . . well . . . infer.

If—no, when—he could pry her away from the loafers, the drifters, the cowboys, and the ne'er-do-wells.

Today.

Arnie Rasmussen girded his loins, figuratively speaking, and made his way down the aisle toward the front of the church, quite forgetting his parents, who were left far behind.

Chapter Two

"Papa."

"Mm?"

"I need some money, Papa."

The elder Rasmussen took his time about answering. He nibbled the end of a grass sprig, rolled his eyes toward a thunderhead that was building to the west, contemplated people at nearby tables. Finally he turned to his son and with a maddening flash of amusement in his pale eyes grunted a laconic, "Why?"

"Papa," Arnie groaned. "You know why."

"I do?"

"Don't tease the boy, Jens."

"Was I, Marta?"

"You know you were."

"Papa."

Jens Rasmussen chuckled. And reached into his pocket for a silver dollar. "I suppose I should tell you not to spend it all in one place, but—"

"Thank you, Papa." Arnie clutched the coin in his fist and raced away toward the back of the church, where Elder Thomas was standing on the raised porch area, surrounded by all the young people of the congregation.

"All right, everyone, come close, closer now, closer, that's right. You all know what this is about. Buy a dessert and get to share it with whoever made it. Think about that, boys. The

17

girls here not only make lovely conversational companions, they also know how to bake a fine confection, let me tell you.'' Brother Thomas winked at his wife across the heads of the crowd and patted his own ample belly. ''I am speaking from experience here, lads. So bid high. And remember, all the proceeds from the cake auction go toward our summer vacation Bible school. So don't hold back. Dig deep in those pockets, boys. Now, let's start the bidding for this . . . did I say cake auction? Never mind, we'll start with this beautiful dried apple pie anyway . . . baked by . . . who made this one? Thelma Jennings? Excellent . . . now who will offer a bid for this fine pie and Thelma's company to share it with you after?''

Arnie felt his heart begin to race. Katherine's contribution— her mother's really, but Arnie wasn't supposed to know that— was a deep-dish berry cobbler. Not that Arnie would have cared if it was sawdust in brine. The excitement stemmed not from the food but from the presence of Katherine. They could talk at the table then, undisturbed by the other eligible gents. That was the custom. Buy the cake and receive privacy in which to enjoy it. The rule was unwritten but inviolate.

Arnie reached into his pants pocket and fingered the coins there. The dollar his father had given him and thirty-seven cents in savings. That should be more than enough. Even if someone else were competing for Katherine's cobbler, they were unlikely to go over fifty cents. One chilly afternoon last fall Tom Morris and Alec Bain got into a bidding free-for-all over the dimpled smile of Alice Carmichael, and Alice's caramel crumb cake sold for eighty-five cents. That was the all-time record, and people still talked about it. Especially about poor Alec. He'd won the bidding that day, but Tom had won the war, later convincing Alice to accept his proposal of marriage. The two were expected to marry some time in October or early November, although no exact date was yet announced. Alice didn't bring cakes to the auction any longer, and Tom kept his money in his britches nowadays.

''Sold!'' Brother Thomas barked, banging an imaginary gavel onto the porch rail. He pointed into the crowd and said, ''Twenty cents, Reuben. Pay up and claim your prize.'' The prize was a slightly asymmetrical layer cake with yellow frosting and Ruthie Van der Horn. Twenty cents. Reuben paid too much, Arnie thought uncharitably.

"Next item up," Brother Thomas said, "is this deep-dish cobbler still warm from the oven. What kind is it, Kathy? Berry? All right, boys. Who will start the bidding for Kathy Mulraney's cobbler? Can you smell it, fellows? It's mouth-watering good, let me tell you. Arnold Rasmussen, is that your hand I see? What's your bid, son?"

"Fifty cents," Arnie declared loudly enough for everyone to hear. He wanted it understood that he was serious and that no one else need bother to bid. This cobbler—this afternoon—belonged to him.

"And a dime," another voice responded from somewhere to Arnie's left.

"Who is that? I don't know you, sir, but welcome. Was that a bid you were making?"

"That's right, brother. I'm passing through and have been away from my dear mother's cooking for too long. That cobbler looks almighty fine to me, and I've a weakness for the like."

Arnie's height allowed him to look over the heads of the rest of the fellows. The man who'd bid against him was older, in his thirties probably, and was wearing a suit that hadn't come off any general mercantile rack. His hat was a narrow-brim affair that would have looked fine on a city's streets but seemed distinctly out of place here, and his tie was knotted at his throat as tidy as tidy could be. The fellow had a handsomely shaped mustache and slicked-back hair, and looked rich and smug and smarmy. Arnie hadn't ever known just what smarmy meant until he saw this fellow standing there. Then he saw. It fit. All too well.

Arnie looked at the man and took an instant dislike to him. Damn him anyway.

"Sixty cents is the bid," Brother Thomas said. "Going once, going—"

"Sixty-five," Arnie barked, waving his hand to make sure he had Brother Thomas's attention.

"Sixty-five over here now." Brother Thomas pointed.

"And a dime," the fancy-pants traveler said with an insulting smile. He didn't even bother to raise his voice when he said it.

Sixty-five and ten, that made . . .

"Eighty cents," Arnie shouted.

"And a dime."

"A dollar, Brother Thomas, I bid a dollar."

"And a dime."

"Dollar and a quarter."

"And a dime."

"A dollar, uh, a dollar thirty-seven." It was all he had. Literally. Arnie began to feel the heat gather under his collar.

"And a dime," the fancy man droned contemptuously.

"A dollar forty-seven is the bid," Brother Thomas said without enthusiasm. "It's up to you, Arnie. What do you say?"

Arnie had no choice. He shook his head, spun, and ran away, clean out of the churchyard and on down the road.

Damn that fellow anyway. He'd ruined everything. Everything.

Chapter Three

There it was again, the red cow with the liver-spotted patch of white on its left side. That was the wildest dang old cow he'd ever seen, near about, and the miserable old thing was teaching its calf to be as wild as it was.

Arnie rode past the brush thicket like he hadn't seen a thing, crossed over to the other side of the draw well below the place where the cow was hiding, and loped up the other side and over the ridge. Only when he was well out of sight of the slab-sided old bitch did he rein his horse back parallel to the ridge-line.

He went far enough that he was sure he would be past the spot where he'd seen the cow, then he once again wheeled left and came sneaking slow and easy over the ridge. Down below him and to his left was the place where . . . aw, dang it. No cow. The old scag and her calf were nowhere to be seen now and . . . there! Way off to the right, toward the head of the shallow draw. The two of them popped out into the open just long enough to scamper up and over the ridgeline and away out of sight. Now how in the world had the damned old cow known . . .

"Arnie. That you, Arnie?"

Arnie pulled his horse to a stop and stared. That kind of explained what happened to the cow, didn't it? Leroy Jordan and Barry Scheer were down there in the shade where the cow had been. Apparently the two of them had come down into

21

the draw behind Arnie and spooked the old liver-spotted cow into the next county. Darn it. Papa would've been mighty pleased if Arnie had been able to get a rope on that calf and brand it, even more so if he could've gotten the calf home so they could pen it and gentle it some. Bad habits, Papa always said, have a way of multiplying, in boys and bovines alike. At least where that damned old cow was concerned, Arnie thought his papa was right.

"What're you boys doing here?" Arnie asked as he turned his horse toward Leroy and Barry. He stopped beside them—the shade felt pretty good at that, and he hadn't hardly taken a break since he left the house just around dawn-thirty this morning—and lifted one leg to drape it over his saddle horn. His horse stood head down and ears limp, looking about as grateful for the rest as Arnie felt.

"Found some tracks that looked like twelve, fourteen head of our stuff took to drifting onto your place. You haven't seen them, have you?"

Arnie shook his head. "No, but I'll push them back your way if I do."

Leroy nodded and pulled the makings out of his shirt pocket. He offered the cloth bag first to Barry, who accepted, and then to Arnie, who didn't.

"No vices, Arnie? That must be awful dull."

"Oh, I reckon I'm about as sinful as a fella needs to be," Arnie returned with a grin, not choosing to take offense.

"Yeah, but I bet you wish you'd had a chance to do some sinning with your neighbor while you still could have," Barry put in.

"What d'you mean by that?"

"You know. Cormac Mulraney's eldest, Katherine."

"What about her?"

"You didn't hear? Jeez, Arnie, where've you been, hiding in a barn someplace? It's the talk of the town, let me tell you."

"What is?" Arnie demanded.

"Katherine Mulraney is. She up and run off with some fella. Guy by the name of . . . what was it, Leroy?"

"Chance," Leroy said. "Isn't that a fancy name for a fancy fellow, though. Chance Martingale. That's the name he gave at the boarding house anyway. Chance. Funny damned name is all I can say.''

''Never mind about him,'' Arnie exploded. ''What about Katherine?''

''Just what we told you, dammit. She run off with this Chance Martingale.''

''This is . . . what? Friday? Wednesday night it would have been,'' Barry said. ''Wednesday afternoon she told her folks Chance was picking her up for a drive down along the creek. She packed a picnic basket and drove off with him in Mr. Dunsmoore's buggy that he'd rented for the evening, and neither her nor him has been seen since. The buggy was left at the crossroads, down by the letter tree, along with a note saying whose rig it was and would the next person going that way please bring it back to Alder Creek with them. Her folks are fit to be tied, of course. Now everybody is saying the girl was no good to begin with and claiming they seen it all along. But I don't really think that's so. I mean, I sure never saw that in her. But you, Arnie, I recall you always been real sweet on her. Tell me the truth, Arnie. Did you have yourself a piece of that before she run off?''

Arnie let out a roar of mixed rage and anguish and flung himself straight off his saddle and onto Barry Scheer before Barry knew up from down.

Chapter Four

"God bless you, one and all," Brother Spense concluded his benediction, and the congregation began filing out. Arnie fidgeted, shifting his weight from one foot to the other, twisting his fingers together, in general acting like a five-year-old who had to use the outhouse.

"Papa."

"Mm?"

"I'm going to go get the horse ready. Is that all right?"

"The horse is just fine, son. You can stand to wait another minute for your mother."

"Yes, sir." But it wasn't easy. The Mulraneys hadn't been at service this morning. That wasn't like them. It was the shame of Katherine running off like that, of course. That had been the main topic of conversation before church today and no doubt the backbiting and catfighting were even worse yesterday, when practically everybody in Prairie County would have been in town to shop. Arnie considered himself—and a lot of other fellows too—awfully lucky to have avoided having to listen to it.

"Papa."

"Yes?"

"Would it be all right if you and Mama go home without me this afternoon?"

"You don't have a way home if we take the buggy and leave you here, Arnold."

24

"I can borrow a horse from Charlie Rhoads," Arnie said. "He won't mind."

There was an agonizing pause. Then Jens Rasmussen nodded, his expression solemn. "All right, son. But don't be late. And don't ask the Mulraneys to feed you. They don't need anyone intruding on their privacy right now."

"How did you—?"

"How could we not know?"

"I won't be late, Papa."

"No, don't be rushing off now. Wait until your mother comes out. You can give her a kiss good-bye before you leave. The Mulraneys will still be there."

"Yes, sir." Arnie remained rooted in place, continuing to fidget and squirm in his anxiety to get away.

Cormac Mulraney was a man as dry and flinty as the land he tried to farm. He gave Arnie a look that was filled with suspicion, but in the end he relented. He nodded abruptly and said, "At least it isn't gloating you've come for, Rasmussen. The others maybe, but not you."

Clarissa Mulraney, the littlest of the Mulraney girls, appeared briefly in the doorway behind her father, then scampered away. Her place was taken a few moments later by her mother, who carried a damp dish towel and a kindly look. "Move aside, mister, so the young man can come in. Have you had your dinner, Arnold? We've finished ours but there is plenty left over. You are welcome to it."

"No, ma'am, thank you."

"Come in anyway. You'll have some milk?"

"I . . . yes'm, thanks." Papa hadn't said anything about accepting a mite to drink. That should be all right.

Old Cormac scowled, but he moved out of the way and Arnie took his hat off and wiped his boots clean on a rag rug laid out before the doorway. Then he followed Mrs. Mulraney in and accepted the stool she showed him to.

As he passed by her, Mrs. Mulraney laid a fingertip under his jaw and turned his chin to the light. She clucked in sympathy at the bruises that discolored Arnie's face courtesy of Barry Scheer and Leroy Jordan, but she said nothing. Arnie guessed she'd either heard about the fight or at least understood without having to be told how those bruises managed to get there.

The Mulraney place wasn't near as proud and well put together as Arnie's mother's frame ranch house. The Mulraneys still lived in what was essentially a large cabin, three rooms down and a loft above. The girls, there were five of them counting Katherine, all slept in the loft. Their parents had a bedroom at one end and there was a kitchen on the other end. The middle was parlor, sitting room, and music room combined, most of it taken up by a battered old piano and beside it a small harp. Those were the heart of the Mulraney home.

Arnie was seated in the parlor, and Annie Mulraney, the next oldest to Katherine, brought him a glass of milk that was foamy with rich cream and still warm from the cow. None of the cream had been removed from it yet, so it had the faintly smoky flavor that Arnie loved.

"If you've come to speak of Katherine, Arnold, don't," Mr. Mulraney warned. "An unruly child is an abomination. We no longer know her. I will listen to no talk about her. She is no longer our concern."

"But I wanted to ask . . . sir, I have to tell you that I don't believe it. That's what I came to tell you, Mr. Mulraney. I don't believe all the things they're saying about Katherine. I don't believe a word of it."

"You don't believe she is gone, Arnold?"

"That isn't . . . sir, I don't believe she ran off with that fella."

Mulraney sniffed and looked away. "She is gone, Arnold. You have to accept that."

"But, sir, I don't . . . I can't . . . believe she went off of her own free will. That's what I mean. I think she was taken."

"Kidnapped, you mean?"

"I don't know how exactly. Taken prisoner or given drugs or whatever. I wouldn't know about that. But I've given this an awful lot of thought, you see. I'm convinced she never would've run off without . . . something. A note, a word, some sort of good-bye to you and her sisters. I think she was taken, sir. I don't believe none of the things the people in town are saying.''

"She is gone, Arnold. That is what we know for sure. She waved good-bye and drove away and no one has seen her since. She took up with that fancy-talking man, and she soiled herself, soiled this entire family. We'll not thank her for that, let me tell you. Her sisters will pay a bitter price for that girl's wickedness, and that is a terrible thing for a man to have to say about his own get, but it is the simple truth and there's no avoiding truth. The girl is an abomination, and her soul will burn in the fires of Hell.'' The old man was stiff and uncompromising in his judgment. There was no doubting that, Arnie saw. No doubt at all.

"You can't blame her, Mr. Mulraney, if Katherine was taken against her will.''

"She was not. She went with that man of her own free will, which the Lord God in His wisdom gives us to use for good or for ill. She chose the path of perdition and it is for that that she will be judged. If you believe otherwise, young Arnold, it is because you do not want to accept the truth. But accept it or no, you cannot change that which is true. Now finish your milk, son, and go home. Forget you ever knew the girl. As we must.'' Mulraney stood and walked away, out into the yard and on toward the half-walled sod dugout that once served as the family's home and now was Mulraney's tool and storage shed.

"He's wrong, you know. Katherine wouldn't do the things they said,'' Arnie insisted uncomfortably.

He looked at Mrs. Mulraney and saw that Katherine's mother was crying, either for the daughter she'd lost or for the harshness of her husband. Arnie did not try to guess which of the two would be the greater vexation. He gulped down the rest of his milk and returned the empty glass to Mrs. Mulraney. Quickly he blurted out a perfunctory thank-you and then fled the Mulraney household.

Katherine had been taken away against her will. Arnie believed that with all his heart.

The question was, what could he do about it when it was so obvious that no one else was going to lift a finger, neither to save her nor to defend her.

But somebody had to, dammit. Somebody had to.

Chapter Five

"Papa, I have to go away for a while."

"I'm sorry, Arnie. I know what you want to do. I understand all that, but I can't allow it."

"But, Papa—"

Jens Rasmussen looked up from the book he'd been reading and stopped his son with a sharp glance. "We have too much work to do here. I can't let you go." Jens permitted himself a small smile. "You know I'd have to hire two men to take your place. I count on you, Arnie. I need you here. And that is apart from the foolishness of your plan. She is a pretty girl, son, but she is not yours. She never was yours, and now she isn't even worthy of . . ." Jens saw the anger rush into his son's expression and abandoned that line of reasoning. "I am sorry, Arnold. No, you cannot leave. Period. We'll not discuss it further." He pulled his gaze away from his son and pretended to concentrate again on the book that lay open in his lap.

"Just like that?" Arnie demanded.

"Just like that," Jens said without looking up again. He turned a page, as yet unread, and adjusted the set of the reading glasses on the bridge of his nose.

"Yes, sir. Thank you, sir." Arnie stood, his posture stiff with anger, and left the room at a slow, controlled pace. His face was wooden and his jaw firmly set.

*   *   *

29

Arnie shivered. He was not sure if that was a response to the chill of the night air . . . or to the enormity of what he knew he had to do.

In all his twenty years, Arnold Rasmussen had never defied his father's will. Not, at least, like this. This was serious. It was also, he reminded himself as he snugged his front cinch tight, necessary.

He patted Baldy on the shoulder and dragged the stirrup off the seat of his scratched and scarred old saddle. He checked the back cinch; it hung loosely away from the horse's belly but was tight enough to keep the back end of the rimfire saddle from rising too far if they should happen to get into a jam. Not that Arnie intended to do any roping today, but then habits are hard to ignore, whether they make any sense or not.

He picked up his bedroll, a thick sausage of canvas and quilts stuffed extra full with two changes of underwear, two changes of socks, two fresh shirts, and Arnie's Sunday suit, and tied it behind the cantle. He used a length of twine to make a loop that he tied to the trigger guard of the shotgun his father had given him for his sixteenth birthday, and draped that over the horn of his saddle. The shotgun was one of the few things that Arnie could consider to be genuinely his own. The shotgun, his clothing, and Baldy, who had pretty much always been Arnie's. One thing was sure, though. He intended to leave with nothing that was not indisputably his to take. It was one thing to leave without Papa's permission. It would have been unconscionable to leave as a thief.

Hobbles and a picket rope already dangled from the strings on his saddle skirt and Baldy's halter would go there too. On the other side of the saddle hung a hemp catch rope, another habit, albeit probably an unnecessary one. He was just about ready.

Arnie untied Baldy and led the brown horse to the door leading out into the ranch yard. It was time, he supposed.

He held the steel and sweet copper bit in his hand for a moment to warm the metal before putting it into Baldy's mouth, then exchanged bit and bridle for rope and halter and, carefully coiling the lead rope, tied them onto a saddle string too.

That about did it. He shivered again, certain this time that it was the predawn coolness that caused it. After all, even though summer was upon them, at that time of day it was cold enough that he could see his breath in the watery gray luminescence that preceded the first hints of the daylight that was to come.

Arnie hesitated for a moment. He felt something—a knot clenched tight in his belly, a lump lodged deep in his throat—that made him reluctant to make this final break.

If he went back inside now, got the note back and burned it . . . No, dammit. He couldn't do that.

Katherine needed him. The whole of Alder Creek was against her, just about. Everyone but Arnie. She needed him now. Wherever she was, Katherine needed him.

He would find her. He would rescue her. And then, why, then she would know that Arnie was the one who cared most for her of all the people there were; she would know that he was the only one who was really and truly right for her.

He would find her and she would know.

Arnie pulled the barn door closed behind him and latched it so it could not blow open when the morning breeze came up, as it likely would in another hour or two.

Then, the lump still big in his throat, he stepped into his stirrup and swung onto Baldy.

Arnie leaned his weight forward just the least bit and Baldy lurched into motion, awkward for those first few steps but then lifting his gait past a walk and falling into the smooth road jog that was so comfortable to ride.

Arnie did not look back as he and Baldy rode away from the house and ranch.

Chapter Six

" 'Lo, Arnie, what brings you all the way down here?" The stagecoach driver hauled his team to a grateful stop. The horses dropped their heads and blew snot, standing hipshot and sweaty in the heat of the late-morning sun.

"Hello, Mr. Barrett. Were you driving the coach last . . . what would it have been? Thursday, I suppose?"

"Of course I was, Arnie, just like always." Barrett puffed his chest out a bit and grinned. "Haven't missed a day of work in more than two years, y'know. Not for any reason."

"Did Miss Mulraney and that fancy-dressed gent ride south with you, Mr. Barrett?"

"Oh, so that's what you want t'know, is it? Well, I know you better than to think you're like them dirty-talking boys in town, Arnie, so I expect you have a good reason to ask?"

"Yes, sir, I surely do."

"You mind telling me what that reason would be?"

Arnie stared down toward the toe of his right boot. It had a smear of mud on it that looked like the outline of a duck right down to the beak and webbed feet. The duck's tail, if it had one, was hidden beneath the wooden curve of his stirrup.

"Never mind," Barrett said. "I heard talk in town about you and the girl."

Arnie flashed a look of sudden hostility.

"No, dammit, not that kind of talk. Nothing bad, just . . . it wasn't nothing bad about the girl."

32

Arnie cleared his throat. He felt embarrassed, but determined to go ahead with this anyway. He just absolutely had to know. "Will you tell me, please?"

"The two of them flagged me down here just like you done today, Arnie. The Mulraney girl and some man I remember driving up from Cheyenne the week before. I didn't know his name at the time, although they tell me now that it's Martingale."

"Yes, sir, that's what I heard too," Arnie said.

"There was a light driving rig tied over by the letter tree there." Barrett pointed to the withered and dying old cottonwood where for a generation or more folks passing by had posted notices and letters and messages to be carried along by others traveling in an appropriate direction. The tree was no longer very often used for that purpose, not since regular mail delivery came to Alder Creek and the neighboring communities, but the name continued. "Martingale paid for two fares back south to Cheyenne. They had his carpetbag and a wicker basket that I expect held her things. They rode with me on down to Cheyenne, and I haven't seen them since. Don't have any idea where they could have got to, if that's what you want to know."

"No, sir, not exactly. What I . . . Mr. Barrett, I just don't believe that Miss Mulraney would have gone off with that man . . . not the way people say, anyhow . . . not of her own free and unfettered will. I think she was mayhap drugged or . . . I don't know. How did she look to you, Mr. Barrett? How did she sound?"

The coach driver scowled in thought and dug a finger into his ear while he did so. After a bit he shrugged. "Near as I can recall, son, the girl never said nothing. Not a word that I could hear. She just kind of stood there and let the man do all the talking, what little of it there was. Martingale told me where they wanted to go, like I said, then he paid the two fares and held the door for the girl to climb up into the coach. I never heard anything else from them the whole trip down. I had three other passengers that day and they may've spoke to them, but I wouldn't know anything about that."

"Did Miss Mulraney look, well, drugged or . . . anything like that, sir?"

Barrett scratched himself and shifted position on the hard bench of his driving seat. He belched softly, then said, "No, I wouldn't say that she did, son. I'm sorry."

"But you said she never said nothing to you. Could she have been drugged or . . . or scared or something?"

"I really couldn't say, Arnie."

"Do you recall who any of those other passengers were, Mr. Barrett?"

"No, I don't. Three traveling men. I don't generally pay that much attention to who's down below. I'm sorry."

"Yes, sir. Thank you, sir."

Barrett gathered up his driving lines. When he took up the slack, his horses' heads came up and their ears tilted forward. They'd had their blow and looked ready to go again. "Tell your father I said hello, Arnie."

"Yes, sir. Thank you, sir." Arnie decided there was no point in mentioning that it probably would be a very long time before he saw or spoke with his father again.

Barrett winked at the younger man and with a flourish set his team into motion.

Arnie sat atop Baldy in the shade of the letter tree and set his eyes toward the south. But it was not Barrett and the stage-coach that he saw when he looked toward distant Cheyenne.

Katherine was innocent. He knew that. And somewhere out there she was alone and frightened. Wherever she was she needed him. Somewhere, somewhere in Cheyenne . . . ?

Chapter Seven

Arnie had never been to Cheyenne before. In truth Arnie had never been much of anyplace before, just Alder Creek and out on the big grass and a couple of times over to the Big Horn Mountains. If that counted for anything, which he didn't suppose it should.

Every fall when the beeves were shipped and every spring when the culls were gotten rid of, Arnie begged his father to be allowed to go along with the bunch, down to the shipping pens at Cheyenne with the rest of the boys. Every fall and without fail every spring as well, Arnie was told—he knew the speech by heart, practically—that it wouldn't be right to leave some hired stranger at home with Mama to help her with all that needed doing around the place and so it was up to Arnie to stay behind and tend to things. "Who can your mother and me count on, son, if not our own? You stay back for now, Arnold. Your time will come. You'll see."

Well, Arnie guessed this was his time to see the city lights, because there Cheyenne was.

He'd never been there, but finding it was no problem. Just follow the road and there it had to be. Or, going cross-country, all a fellow had to do was ride south to the railroad tracks and turn left. He would get to Cheyenne by and by.

And there, sure as shooting, it was.

Big. Bigger than Arnie expected.

Not that he was so very certain sure just what it was that

35

he'd expected. But this wasn't it. This was bigger. But more than that it was . . . busier.

Not only did Cheyenne sprawl all over the place—it was said that several thousand folks lived here in this one town—but there was a liveliness about it that Alder Creek couldn't match.

Cheyenne fair bustled. There were drays and men on horseback and men afoot and chattering women and open storefronts . . . and open saloons too, beckoning the weary and the thirsty to come inside, and . . . and he didn't know what all else.

A train engine, the first he'd ever seen, although of course he'd seen many and many a picture of them, sat puffing and hissing beside a handsome, low-roofed building with a big sign on the end of it proclaiming that this was indeed CHEYENNE, POP. 3,487.

Arnie's eyes like to goggled when he saw that. More than three thousand souls, all of them living in this one spot. Incredible.

Alder Creek had, what? Two hundred? Two hundred fifty? It couldn't be any more than that, and likely was less. No wonder Cheyenne was the territorial capital, Arnie thought as he and Baldy came closer and closer to the busy street that ran parallel to the Union Pacific tracks.

The huge locomotive let out a burst of steam and an ear-splitting shriek of noise, and poor Baldy like to went out of his skin. He squatted in sudden alarm and jumped sideways away from the engine, and for the next little bit Arnie was pretty thoroughly occupied with hanging on tooth and toenail and trying to regain his seat, for most of him was hung off to one side of the saddle while poor Baldy tried his level best to get gone from this thing that was after him.

Arnie clung tight and wasn't too proud to grab leather, and that was the only thing that saved him from the humiliation of entering Cheyenne while being dragged by his own stirrup. Or worse, entering Cheyenne on foot while Baldy loped for home without him.

Eventually Arnie got the horse calmed down and his own backside on the seat where it belonged, and he put Baldy into a jog, wanting to get that loudmouth steam engine as far behind them as was reasonable.

"I thought sure you was taking a dust bath back there, fella," a friendly cowboy said as Arnie came near. "Nice riding to stay on top of 'im."

"Thanks," Arnie said with a grin. He guided Baldy over to the sidewalk where the cowboy was and politely stepped down to the ground. "You wouldn't be able to tell me where I might find someone here, would you, neighbor?"

"A drink or a fancy girl or the loading pens, I can point you toward any o' them," the cowboy said. "Is it somebody in particular you're wanting?"

"Ayuh, it is," Arnie told him.

"Somebody that lives here?"

Actually Arnie did not know. This Chance Martingale could be from anyplace. Including Cheyenne. "I . . . I ain't sure," he admitted.

"Tell you what. If this fella you want is local, the town marshal might know him or know of him. If he's passing through, ask at the hotels. There aren't so many of them that you couldn't hit them all in one afternoon."

Arnie thought that over for a moment, then nodded. "Thanks. I should have thought of those things my own self, shouldn't I?"

The cowboy shrugged. "No harm done."

Arnie stepped back onto Baldy and the cowboy told him, "Good luck to you."

"And t'you, neighbor."

"See you around, okay?"

Arnie touched the brim of his hat and reined Baldy down the street. Lordy, but this was one busy place. But surely someone here would know where Katherine was. Surely someone would remember seeing a girl so fine and pretty as Katherine.

Why, all he had to do, probably, was find the town marshal and then go fetch Katherine away from that sonuvabitch Martingale. They could work out later on if Katherine wanted charges filed against the kidnapper or if it would be better to leave things be so that she didn't have to testify to anything in open court that might, well, sully her fine reputation.

Yeah, they could think about stuff like that later on.

Arnie bumped Baldy into a lope in his eagerness to find whoever the Cheyenne marshal was and get this thing over and done with. And get Katherine safely home where she belonged.

Chapter Eight

"Martingale, eh?" the gray-haired and crusty marshal repeated, mouthing the word a couple of times as if the flavor of it might provoke a memory. "Martingale." Marshal Beneke chewed on the name a little more, then shook his head. "Only Martingale I know of, son, is the kind you put onto a horse. Can't say I recall ever meeting a man of that name."

"You're real sure about that, sir?" Arnie persisted. "He's the sort a man might remember. A real fancy city type. Fancy clothes, glittery stickpin in his tie, funny-looking hat with hardly any brim to it and his hair greased down underneath the hat."

Beneke gave Arnie a wan little hint of a smile and shook his head a mite. "Son, we get twenty of that kind through here every day. And no, I'm pretty sure there's no one name of Martingale that lives in town. I'm sure of that because this man would be a potential voter, and I know every man of voting age in this here county. Or know something about him if I haven't yet had the pleasure of making his acquaintance. I can tell you for certain sure there's no one named Martingale on the voting rolls here."

Arnie was disappointed. He'd been so hopeful. . . .

"What about a young lady named Katherine Mulraney?" he asked. He would have preferred to keep Katherine out of the conversation, which was why he hadn't brought her up to begin with.

39

"I know of a Cletus Mulraney who lives over on—"

"No, sir. I mean, I apologize for interrupting you, but Katherine doesn't live here. I know that. She comes from Alder Creek and . . ."

"Alder Creek," Beneke mouthed aloud without waiting for Arnie to finish. "That where you're from, son?"

"Yes, sir, it is."

"And this Mulraney girl, she run off with Martingale, did she?"

"No, sir," Arnie protested, a bit of heat in his voice. "She wouldn't run off with no slicker like him. She was kidnapped, Marshal."

Beneke coughed into his fist and seemed to give that accusation some thought. "I see," he said after a few moments. "Sure of that, are you?"

"Yes, sir, I'm sure of it."

Beneke swiveled his desk chair first to one side and then to the other. He steepled his fingers beneath his chin and leaned back, not looking at Arnie when he spoke again. "You know, son . . . and I'm not saying this is what happened in your girl's case, mind; I'm not saying that at all . . . but what happens sometimes is that a girl who is, shall we say, not too sophisticated in the ways of folks, a girl who may have been protected from ugliness by her family, a girl like that can get bored with small-town living and farm or ranch life, and she gets to be an easy target for smooth-talking fellas with nice clothes and a pocket full of money. Sometimes a girl finds herself talked into, well, into doing whatever it is the fellow wants from her. Generally not the sort of thing she'd want her folks or her friends to know about. If you take my meaning."

Arnie's ears commenced to burn. He knew what the marshal was saying. Of course he did. But that wasn't the way it was with Katherine. Not her. She wouldn't do . . . anything like that. She just wouldn't.

"The thing is, son, once an egg is broke you might as well go ahead and have yourself an omelette, because there's no way on God's green earth you can glue it back together again. Not the way it was to begin with. So if that's what happened with your Miss Mulraney and Mr. Martingale, well, the best thing for you, son, would be to go home and forget about it, because even if you manage to find her it won't be the same sweet girl you used to know. She'd be . . . different, son. Harder and . . . different.''

"It wasn't that way," Arnie snapped, springing to his feet in a burst of anger at the know-it-all old man with a tin star on his chest. "She was kidnapped. I know she was."

"All right, son. I don't know the facts of the case so I won't try and argue with you.''

"Will you help me find her, then?" Arnie demanded.

"No, I won't.''

"But you said—"

"If your county sheriff sends me a Want order or somebody shows me a warrant for the arrest of Martingale . . . or just tells me to be on the lookout for your Miss Mulraney . . . then I'll undertake due process. But I won't go out interfering in the lives of private citizens, son. Not on your say-so alone. I'm sorry.''

"You're a sad excuse for a town marshal," Arnie accused as a wave of sudden heat began to build up behind his eyes.

"I understand how you would feel that way, young man, and I want you to know that I take no offense.''

"I intend offense, damn you," Arnie blurted as the stinging in his eyes grew worse and his vision became dimmed and watery.

The marshal pretended not to see, peering off into a corner of his office instead.

There was nothing more Arnie could accomplish there anyway. He spun about and ran headlong into the street, rushing right past Baldy in his desire to get the hell away from that smug son of a bitch Beneke.

Chapter Nine

Arnie was discouraged. Tired, disgusted, and discouraged. He had already been to every hotel in Cheyenne, even the one south of the railroad tracks that would give cheap shelter to Mexicans and Negroes and Chinese. No one seemed to know a man named Chance Martingale. No one admitted to having seen a girl like Katherine Mulraney.

Yet Martingale had brought Katherine here to Cheyenne just last week. Mr. Barrett said so. He gave them passage south in his coach and let them off at the stage depot. That's what he'd said. That's what he'd told Arnie with his very own mouth. So Arnie knew good and well Katherine and that Martingale fellow had been here.

Arnie sighed. The question was where they'd gone once they'd left the . . . he stopped practically in mid stride and snapped his fingers. Of course. The stage depot. Arnie stopped his morose pacing and swung onto Baldy. Maybe someone at the stagecoach office would remember Katherine. Or at least maybe someone there knew or remembered Martingale.

"Martingale? No, I don't recall anyone by that name," the balding clerk in the Tifton Brothers Express office said. "Of course you should realize that I don't often know the names of my passengers, not even the regulars. They come in and put down their money and I give them a ticket, and for the most part that's that. Sometimes they'll have a company

42

voucher to pay with and then I know who they represent if not who they are themselves.''

"Represent," Arnie repeated.

"That's right. The company they work for, I mean. The regulars, most of them, aren't traveling for themselves, they're working for a company, selling something or whatever, and the company pays for their tickets, either with a voucher that their company arranges with Tifton Brothers or else they take back a cash receipt and are repaid their travel expenses.''

"I see," Arnie said. The idea of someone else, a company or whatever, paying for someone's travel was something he had never encountered before nor had any reason to think about. Until now.

"As for passengers arriving," the Tifton Brothers clerk went on, "I don't generally even see them. They get off the coach and collect their gear and away they go. No reason for them to come in here unless they're buying tickets to go on. And that sure wouldn't be normal, since Cheyenne is the southern terminus for our line. Passengers coming here usually have business right here or else they're going on by rail." He rather proudly added, "From Cheyenne, you know, you can reach anyplace from San Francisco to New York City and almost anything in between.''

That thought was not one that Arnie found particularly cheering. By now he supposed Katherine could actually *be* in San Francisco. Or in New York.

"Martingale could be one of your regulars," Arnie said hopefully, and went on to describe the sleazy SOB for the helpful clerk.

The Tifton Brothers representative shrugged. "I'm sorry, but half the traveling men who use our coaches on their routes could fit that description. Is there anything else you can think of that might help pin him down to one person in particular?''

Arnie frowned and tried to think. But all he really remembered about that Sunday afternoon was how awfully pretty Katherine had been. Martingale just hadn't made that much of an impression. Not at the time, he hadn't. "He's a slick talker," was all Arnie could think of. "He has a way with words.''

Frank Roderus

The clerk laughed. "That information adds in the other half of my regulars. Salesmen. They're all slick talkers. It's their stock in trade. Sorry."

Arnie sighed again.

"Have you tried asking at the hotels?" the clerk suggested. "Most of the traveling men, at least those that cover a regular route, they get set into habits, stay at the same places, eat at the same cafes. They kind of like familiarity when they're on the road like that. I think it makes them feel more to home, like."

"I've already done that," Arnie said.

"How about the boarding houses, then? Some of the men like a boarding house instead of a hotel."

Arnie brightened. "He stayed at a boarding house when he was in Alder Creek," he said. Civic pride kept him from mentioning that Alder Creek had no actual hotel of its own, although a couple of the saloons offered rooms. With or without overnight companionship. Not that Arnie knew about that first hand. But he'd heard plenty. Oh yes, he'd heard plenty about the sort of women who worked in those saloons. Ugly, sick, diseased things, those women were. Arnie knew. He'd heard all about their kind.

"Well then," the clerk chirped, "that's it. You need to ask at the boarding houses. And don't worry. If your man is a regular visitor in Cheyenne, someone will know him. Just keep looking."

"Yes, sir. Thank you, sir." Arnie touched the brim of his hat and went back outside. It was getting late in the day and his stomach was beginning to grumble at the way he'd been neglecting it lately. Probably Baldy would have been grumbling too if he'd been able. Arnie decided he had best postpone finding Martingale—and Katherine—one more day. Tomorrow he would ask at the boarding houses in Cheyenne.

And by tomorrow night, well, by tomorrow night maybe he would have Katherine safe and on her way home again.

Why shoot, he thought, he should have asked at the Tifton Brothers office about their northbound schedule. After all, he would need a way to get Katherine home again once he found her.

44

Chapter Ten

A dollar and thirty-seven cents. The same dollar thirty-seven he'd had when he tried to buy that cobbler at the church auction. Funny how it had seemed so much then and so little now, but it was all the cash money he had. And it sure wasn't going to stretch far at city prices.

He could hire a hotel room for himself and a stall for Baldy. But that would leave him without any extra to eat on tonight or tomorrow morning.

He could take a cheap flop in the canvas-roofed rathole across the tracks, but that would only mean he and Baldy could eat as well as having a place to lie down.

Or he could . . . jeez, he wasn't sure what else his choices might be.

What he needed was more money.

No, what he needed was to find Katherine and get the hell home where both of them belonged.

At home in Alder Creek it wouldn't matter that his pockets were near to empty. At home he could go to any business in town or for that matter to just about any house in town and they'd see that he got whatever it was that he needed, food or shelter or any dang thing.

But this wasn't home, was it? And here he didn't know a soul.

For the first time in his life Arnie felt alone.

Oh, he'd been by himself aplenty. Out on the grass looking

for cattle. Away hunting or fishing. Stuff like that. He'd been alone for days on end sometimes. But that was different. Here in Cheyenne he was surrounded by folks. And yet he felt more alone than he'd ever felt before.

He thought it over and just to make sure counted his money again, but there wasn't any more of it now than there had been to start with. It was still just a dollar and thirty-seven cents, and he knew that wouldn't carry him and Baldy too awfully far.

Eventually he decided his best bet was to go ahead and act like he was the same sort of alone that he was comfortable and familiar with.

He found a general mercantile and for fifteen cents bought himself a can of sardines, a can of peaches, a walnut-sized pinch of ready-ground Arbuckle's, and a poke of hard-baked, salt-top crackers. Which took care of his needs. Sardines and crackers for supper, peaches and crackers for breakfast come morning, and the bit of coffee to wash it all down. That should do just fine, for a man doesn't really need near as much as he tends to pack into himself most of the time. Arnie had made do on less than that many and many a time while caught out working cows. As for Baldy's supper and a place for the both of them to sleep, well, that should work out too.

Arnie stepped onto his saddle and pointed Baldy away from the bustle of downtown Cheyenne. There was still plenty of grass in Wyoming, and Arnie figured to make use of it.

"Come up slow and easy, you, and don't be thinking about reaching for the gun I see on the ground there. I got mine already cocked and aimed, and you wouldn't have a chance."

Arnie felt a chill fill his belly and practically stop his heart in its tracks.

He was awake now. Lordy, he reckoned he was. Awake and scared and unsure just what was going on here.

In the dim moonlight he could see a figure towering above him, the man's form a black silhouette hard against the starlit night sky.

True to his word, the man had a gun in hand, and the revolver was tipped downward so that its aim was more or less focused on Arnie's bedroll.

"Mister," Arnie blurted, "I ain't got enough money to be worth robbing. Honest, I don't."

"This is no robbery. Now ease away from that long gun like I just told you."

The misery in Arnie's belly got bigger and colder as he moved aside, rolling out from under his covers and off the bedroll onto the dew-wet chill of the grass where he'd laid his bed.

The gun that was pointed his way moved with him, and Arnie had visions of what all would happen if that revolver went off.

He could practically feel the hot, hard smack of the bullet hitting his stomach and penetrating. Inside him. God, all the way inside his body.

The thought was enough to make him sick, and for a moment there Arnie was sure he was going to puke. Actually for a moment there he didn't much care if he puked or not. He was that scared. Except if he did, he would likely spew all over the man with the gun, and then what would happen? Probably the guy would shoot, whether he intended to or not, and everything Arnie was so scared of would come true.

God!

"Please don't shoot, mister, please." Arnie felt close to crying. At the moment he didn't care about that either, didn't care if this awful stranger with the gun saw him cry or not. What mattered was that the man not shoot. "Please, mister. Please."

"Who are you, boy? You sound about half familiar."

Arnie told him. Quick.

"Oh, jeez," the man blurted. "Rasmussen?"

"Yes, sir."

"This is Marshal Beneke, son. You remember me?"

"Y-yes, sir."

Beneke lowered the hammer of his revolver to a safe position and dropped the gun back into the belt pouch where he carried it. Arnie felt—literally—weak with relief when he saw the marshal do that. "What the hell are you doing here, son?" Beneke demanded.

"I didn't have money enough for a hotel, sir, and this spot alongside the creek is empty. I mean, nobody is using it for anything. So I just kinda thought—"

"You aren't out in the country now, Rasmussen. You can't just throw your bed wherever you feel like it here, son."

"But there's nobody around and I thought—"

"I know what you thought, but you can't act like that here. That's what I'm trying to tell you, son. This is the city, and the land hereabouts is private owned. You see what I'm saying? You know why I'm here now?"

Arnie shook his head, then realized the marshal might not be able to see too well in the darkness and said, "No, sir, I surely don't."

"The man that owns this land saw your fire or your horse or something, and he turned in a complaint against you. He asked me to arrest you and put you in jail overnight on a charge of trespass. That means being on private property without the owner's permission. Do you hear me, son?"

"Yes, sir, but—"

"No, don't be giving me any 'but' talk. You set up your camp on somebody's land without his say-so. And that, son, is against the law."

"Sir, I didn't mean—"

"Oh, I know you didn't mean anything wrong here. You didn't know any better. Last night. Now you do." The marshal shook his head and stared off toward the stars for a few seconds, then he sighed and looked back down at Arnie, who was sitting cross-legged—his backside becoming soaked with cold dew—on the grass. "I tell you what, Rasmussen. The man that owns this pasture is a friend of mine. I'll square it with him that you can sleep here the rest of tonight. Hell, that's only for a few more hours anyhow. But don't you come back here tomorrow night."

"Yes, sir. Thank you, sir." Arnie meant that. More or less. He still didn't quite have a handle on the idea that a fellow couldn't lay out a bedroll and make himself a fire wherever he found himself come dark. But this didn't seem the proper time to be pondering on it.

The marshal turned as if to leave, then turned back to face Arnie again. "While I think about it, you haven't been drinking any water out of this creek, have you?"

"I made myself some coffee before I turned in. Was that all right?"

"Sort of. Not really."

"Now Marshal, surely that man don't think he owns every drop of water that passes through his land. Why—"

"Whoa, son. It isn't the water you took but what might be in it that I'm warning you against."

"Sir?"

"You're probably all right this time since you boiled the water to make your coffee. But don't drink water from a stream anywhere around a town, son. Don't even use water straight from a creek to wash your plate or spoon. It can make you bad sick, even kill you if you get the runs real bad."

"But the water was moving along nice and quick, and I didn't see no—"

"I know, son, it sounds crazy, but believe me it's true. Water taken up around cities and towns has disease in it. Whatever it is that makes it so is too small for you to see. But even running water isn't safe. Not even ice cold water running so fast you can hear it, even that isn't safe. Believe me, and learn to watch out for yourself. Come morning don't you drink any of this water here. I tell you what, Rasmussen. Come morning you drop by the jail and shake me out if I've gone back to sleep. I'll take you by the best cafe in town and see you have a proper breakfast. And water that'll be safe for you to drink. All right?"

"Yes, sir. Thank you again, sir."

The Cheyenne town marshal said good-night and went off—on foot, Arnie noticed—toward the few lights and the dimly seen shapes of the sleeping city.

Arnie shivered, then crawled back under the covers in an attempt to recapture his disrupted sleep.

Lordy, but things were awfully different here from anything he'd ever known or so much as heard of before now.

Chapter Eleven

"I'm sorry, sonny, he isn't here right now."

"Pardon me?"

"The man you asked about. Mr. C. F. Martingale? I said he isn't here just now."

"But . . . you know him?"

"Certainly. Didn't I just say that?"

Not exactly. But Arnie was not complaining. The tall old woman at the boarding house knew Martingale. Actually knew him. It was amazing. It was wonderful. Arnie's face cracked open in a wide grin. This day was going some kind of fine, wasn't it. His belly was full with a hot meal courtesy of the marshal. And now this. At the second boarding house he'd come to. The lady knew Martingale.

"This is where he lives?" Arnie asked.

"No, but this is where he stays. When he happens to be in town. Which he isn't just now."

The grin disappeared, to be replaced by a frown of mild confusion. "But if this isn't where he lives . . . ?"

The woman shook her head and offered the explanation, "He's a salesman, son. He travels a regular route. Comes through here, oh, once every five weeks, more or less."

"But he isn't here right now," Arnie said as comprehension began to dawn.

"That's right. I haven't seen Mr. Martingale in, I'd say, three weeks or thereabouts."

"You didn't see him last week then?"

"I believe I just said that. He last stayed with me about three weeks back."

Arnie thought about that. It made sense, he supposed. This time through, Martingale had a kidnapped girl with him. The man couldn't hardly take Katherine with him to a boarding house where there would surely be questions asked and suspicions raised. Of course he couldn't. Naturally he would not have stayed there after drugging Katherine and carrying her off from home. Wouldn't bring her there on his next sales trip either. If he took her with him at all. Arnie didn't know what to expect about that. Whatever would Martingale do with Katherine when the man had to go out working again? Lock her up someplace? Not for that amount of time he couldn't.

It occurred to Arnie that he needed to find Katherine almighty soon, before this Martingale went on the road again. God only knew what might happen to Katherine when that time came.

"Do you, um, do you know where I might could find Mr. Martingale?"

"I don't know where he lives, if that's what you mean," the boarding house lady told him. "Denver, I suppose, but he's never said. I know the company he works for is in Denver. They might tell you how to find him."

"And that would be?"

"Hibbing Leather Works," the woman said.

Arnie had heard about that company. They made heavy-duty work harnesses, industrial belting, buggy whips, drover's whips, things like that. "They're in Denver, ma'am?"

"Hibbing is, yes. I couldn't really say about Mr. Martingale. I give him receipts for his room rent whenever he stays with me, and I would assume the company reimburses him for his travel and expenses. Otherwise he wouldn't need the receipts. But as for where Mr. Martingale lives when he's not on the road, I really couldn't tell you." She smiled and volunteered, "Such a nice man, Mr. Martingale is. Is there a message you would like to leave for him? He'll be back in a few more weeks, you know. I would be glad to take a message for him."

Arnie thanked the lady and turned away. He sighed. Martingale and Katherine were not in Cheyenne. He was convinced of that now.

So, logically, Martingale must have taken Katherine with him to Denver. Dammit. Arnie swung onto Baldy and retraced his path back to the marshal's office. He didn't know who else to turn to for advice, and so far Marshal Beneke had done right by him. Maybe the marshal could make some suggestions about what Arnie ought to do next.

This whole affair was awfully confusing, Arnie thought. Just about more than Arnie felt able to handle. But too important to lay back on. Not when he was the only hope of rescue poor Katherine had left.

No, come what may, he would press on.

That was the one thing he was sure of.

Chapter Twelve

"Go home, son," the marshal said, his expression firm and his voice serious. "No, don't look at me like that. I'm giving you the same advice I'd give to my very own son if he was in a fix like this."

"Sir, you don't understand. Katherine was—"

"Rasmussen, I understand a lot more than you think I do. After breakfast this morning I stopped by the telegraph office. I got a wire off to your sheriff up home. He responded right away. Do you know what he tells me, Rasmussen?"

"Sir, I know, but—"

"Don't be rude, son. Listen to me. The girl's very own father says she's no good. Says she ran away with her fancy man of her own free will. Knew what she was doing and did it anyway. The sheriff says her father doesn't want her back, son. Not after, well, whatever it is she's been doing with that fellow since. Now doesn't that tell you anything?"

"What it tells me, sir, is that Mr. Mulraney is wrong. So is the sheriff, sir. I know Katherine. I know she wouldn't do what everyone is saying she done. She was drugged or put in fear of her life or . . . or God knows what else that man might have done to make her go with him. But whatever it was, sir, it wasn't Katherine's fault, and I want to get her away from that fellow."

"Who you say is in Denver now," the marshal said.

"Yes, sir. That's what the lady at the boarding house told me."

"Do you know how big a place Denver is, Rasmussen? Why, Denver makes Cheyenne look small."

"I wouldn't know about that, sir, but the lady told me where Martingale works. I expect I'll be able to find him, and once I do then I'll be able to find Katherine. That's all I care about right now."

"My advice to you stands, Arnie. Given to you with all the good will and sincerity that's in me. Go home, son. Let the girl alone and go back home. It won't be easy for you to forget her, but someday.—"

"I can't do that, sir," Arnie said stubbornly. "I can't let her life be ruined by something that isn't her fault."

Marshal Beneke sighed and shook his head. "I wish I knew the right words to get through to you, Rasmussen. I truly do."

"This is something I have to do, Marshal. I know you mean well. I do understand that, and I thank you. But this is something I really got to do or I won't be able to live with myself after."

Reluctantly the town marshal nodded, adding another sigh afterward. "In that case, Arnie, let me give you a little more advice. And this time try to pay attention, will you? Listen to what I say and at least think about doing what I tell you."

"Yes, sir," Arnie said politely, not at all sure that he meant it, but not wanting to be rude to someone who so obviously did have Arnie's best interests at heart.

Chapter Thirteen

The first part wasn't bad. Arnie'd already thought of it himself, expected it, even prepared ahead of time to do it. After all, that was the reason he'd brought the shotgun along to begin with. Heck, you don't need a bird-shooter inside a city. And it was the only thing of value—well, almost the only thing— that he'd ever owned.

So turning the handsomely made L. C. Smith into cash, as the marshal suggested, was the reason he'd brought it along with him to start with.

And it had gone well enough, he supposed. He knew what the gun was worth and so did the shopkeeper who Marshal Beneke had said was most likely to give him a fair deal. New, the gun would cost twenty-two, even as much as twenty-four dollars. It was an awful fine gun. Papa hadn't skimped when he bought it.

The shopkeeper would sell it used, in good condition, for eleven or twelve dollars. Him and Arnie dickered and talked and lied back and forth a little and in the end the shopkeeper paid over eight dollars for the gun and kicked in another two bits for the Number Six prairie chicken loads that Arnie had no use for once the gun was sold.

Which put money enough in Arnie's pocket for him to get to Denver on and to eat for a couple days. Barely.

But as for the rest of the marshal's advice . . . it made sense. Of course it did once Arnie put some thought to it.

But it hurt. The thought of it hurt so awful bad.

He stood outside the livery stable for fifteen, twenty minutes, thinking there ought to be a way to do something different, ought to be some course he could choose other than this one.

But there wasn't. Not really.

It would cost four dollars and a half to buy a ticket to Denver. Four dollars more if he wanted to pay for stock car space to haul Baldy with him.

That would as good as wipe him out.

Or he could just step into the saddle and ride south. Denver would be easy enough to find. Just get someone to point out which set of rails went there and ride alongside them. He could get to Denver that way. Eventually. But would Chance Martingale . . . and Katherine . . . still be there by the time he could ride the distance by horseback? Maybe, but maybe not. The lady at the boarding house said Martingale made his route every five weeks or so. And it'd been a good four weeks since he'd set out the last time, again according to what the boarding house woman reported. So if it took another five or six days, say, to ride down from Cheyenne . . . and then however much more time to find the harness company and look up Martingale at his home . . . that was cutting things mighty fine. Going to Denver on horseback could mean Arnie would miss finding Martingale and Katherine. He couldn't risk that.

But . . . oh, God . . . what was a man without a horse anyhow?

Arnie couldn't remember—literally had no memory of—any time in his whole life long that he hadn't had a horse to count on.

And most of that time, the best of that time, the horse had been Baldy.

Baldy'd been foaled right there in their own catch pen. Hand-fed and gentled right from his very first day. Pen-raised and special trained. Why, the little horse was as much friend and companion as he was horse. More than those things, maybe.

And now . . .

It was all Arnie could do to hold back the hot, moist feel

inside his eyes as, steeling himself to what had to be done, he took up the reins and led Baldy the last few rods to the doors of the livery.

He felt if the livery man offered to pay thirty pieces of silver for Baldy, Arnie ought to take it. That would be about right for any SOB that would sell off a faithful and trusting friend.

Chapter Fourteen

God, he felt awful. Guilty. Like he'd done something wrong. But then . . . he had. Sort of.

Baldy belonged to somebody else now. The money was in Arnie's pocket, and by now the man at the livery stable likely would have sold him on to someone else. Arnie didn't know who and didn't want to. Better, in fact, that he never find out.

And there wasn't anything wrong with it. So why in hell did he feel so rotten about the whole thing? Like he'd sold an old friend into slavery or something.

After all, it was only a horse. Horses don't know anything. They're stupid and not particularly friendly and don't have any loyalty. Not like a dog does. A dog really cares about its humans. Horses don't. They have habits, sure, but not friendships.

It was only a damned horse.

Good one, though. Baldy had been the best. Arnie remembered . . . He scowled and grumbled silently to himself. It didn't matter what he damn remembered, did it?

Arnie slumped lower in the cinder-pocked seat and tried to work up some excitement about being on a train for the first time. Feeling so bad about Baldy was ruining what should have been a lot of fun. After all, Arnie couldn't remember ever seeing a train before, much less ever having been on one.

And it really was kind of exciting. Or if not exactly exciting then certainly scary. The speed of the huge machine, rushing blindly pell-mell on a course Arnie couldn't see, much less control, made his belly tighten and his parts pucker up.

And the jiggly-bump racketa-racketa-racketa clatter and clack of the car was scary too. It felt like they might bounce off the rails and crash at any moment without warning. He'd read about train crashes. They were supposed to be horrible things, and he could believe that with all the weight and terrible speed. He didn't see how any machine could be trusted to do what it ought to without fail.

The constant, irregular motion frightened and disturbed him and for a long time he sat with his backside bolted firm to the seat, afraid to go to the back of the car where the water barrel and the toilet were. He stayed sitting until he was afraid he was going to wet himself if he stayed sitting any longer and then, worried he wouldn't be able to walk while the train was moving, but more worried about the consequences if he didn't go back there, he got up and wobbled from one handhold to the next, reaching out and grabbing the backs of other folks' seats to steady himself while he tried to sort out how to make his legs work properly while the car was bumping and thumping and rocking from side to side.

Arnie could stick a saddle pretty much regardless of what any horse might have to say about it. But this . . . this was something like he'd never experienced before, and it was awkward and unpleasant and he didn't think he would ever learn to be comfortable on a railroad train. He was sure he didn't want enough experience to ever find out if he could adjust to this.

He stepped down onto the floor about the same time the car hit a bump on the rails, and a lance of pain shot through Arnie's right knee, teaching him to walk without letting his knees lock. After that he discovered it wasn't as bad as he'd first thought, so long as he kept hold of the nearby seat backs.

That probably marked him as a greenhorn, he realized. Kind of like some tenderfoot grabbing for the saddle horn as soon as a tame horse moves out. But so what, dammit. He *was* a greenhorn at this train-riding stuff, and didn't intend ever to be otherwise. Not if he had his way about it.

He made it to the back of the car and suffered through the

ordeal of making water while being bounced and jostled and half suffocated in the process, then went out and helped himself to a cup of water from the barrel to cut some of the dry nervousness out of his throat. He felt a little better after that, even though he knew he'd only completed half of what he'd set out to do. He still had to make it back up the aisle to his seat at the far end of the car. If ever he had to ride another of these contraptions, he told himself, he was dang sure gonna pick a seat at the back end of the car and never mind the stink.

The uniformed conductor came through, ambling along just as smooth and easy as if he'd been walking down the street in Cheyenne, and Arnie cleared his throat and got up nerve enough to stop the man.

"Excuse me, sir. Are we still far from Denver?"

"We're running right on time, sir. Should pull in at two-seventeen. Exactly."

Sir. The man had called him sir. Arnie didn't think—no, he was downright sure of it—no one had ever called him that before. Sir. It sounded strange to him. He would have thought he would feel good about it, but in fact he did not. Odd.

"Thank you," he said softly, and the conductor passed on forward at a casual gait.

Arnie started off behind him with a look of grim determination, still grabbing one seat back after another but now at least with a little confidence that he might return to his seat still alive.

Lordy, but he did wish none of this had had to happen.

Chapter Fifteen

Cheyenne was the biggest place Arnold Rasmussen had ever seen, or so much as imagined.

Cheyenne, Wyoming Territory, wouldn't have made a pimple on the backside of Denver, State of Colorado.

Lordy, there must've been thousands and *thousands* of folks living in Denver.

Why, the smoke from cooking fires alone was enough to practically blot out the sight of the clouds. Or of the mountains, which were even bigger and more rugged and magnificent than the Big Horns that Arnie was familiar with back home.

Here the buildings were made of kiln-fired bricks and dressed stone, and the streets—he'd read about such things—were hard-surfaced with a gritty, black stuff that he guessed was macadam.

Streetcars ran on steel rails like tiny, horse-drawn trains while huge drays and freight wagons and carriages, mostly private but a lot of hacks for hire too, rumbled back and forth to add to the confusion of the traffic.

There was foot traffic too. Lordy, he guessed there was. Gentlemen—no vests and shirtsleeves here; every man was wearing a proper suitcoat and most had ties knotted at their collars as well—and fine ladies in abundance, the ladies wearing bustles to hide their figures and carrying delicate parasols to protect their complexions from the sunlight. People fairly swarmed along the sidewalks. And the sidewalks. Arnie'd never seen the like. There were a few ordinary boardwalks, but most here in Denver seemed to be made of paving blocks, some of brick, and some of some other material, as hard as the macadam but gray rather than black, that he'd never seen before and could not even guess to try and put a name to.

And the buildings. Tall? Four, five stories high, some of them. They reached nigh to the sky, he thought as he walked among them, gawking so that he like to put a cramp in his neck from peering up all the time.

And everywhere he looked there was . . . something. Folks, structures, pavement . . . something. It was like every square foot had to be put to some use or else it might be snatched away. Everything had to be occupied. Why, there was hardly room enough to accommodate a few weeds between the sidewalks and the building fronts.

Arnie shivered. Denver was exciting. That was a fact. But he wasn't sure he liked it overmuch. It was so crowded. So busy. And so *loud*.

People talked. Newsboys shouted. Teamsters cussed. Iron-rimmed wheels crunched and groaned. Iron-shod hooves clattered and traces jangled. Behind Arnie, back toward the Union Pacific depot, a train whistle screamed and another, more distant, answered.

A deep-throated bell clanged and a couple of blocks ahead Arnie saw a bright red fire company wagon flash across an intersection as a band of uniformed men dashed somewhere with their pump and hoses.

Closer by, some children were laughing and playing a game of ring-around-the-rosy in the side yard of a church building. At least that was homely and familiar to him. The sight and the sound of the kids at play helped settle him and made him feel a mite better. There were some things, anyway, that weren't so awfully different between Denver and Alder Creek.

Arnie shivered again and set his jaw against a growing tendency to tremble. He felt about naked there. And mighty lonely, even though he was surrounded by what looked like half the world's entire population.

Just the least bit shaky, Arnie shifted his bundle of belongings—his bedroll and extra clothes all wrapped up tidy and carried in the belly of his saddle with the stirrup leathers and latigo and everything cinched tight to make it all a neat package easily carried—from one shoulder to the other.

There really wasn't much sense in lagging, though. By then it was past the midpoint of the afternoon and soon would be evening time.

With any kind of luck, he still had time that day to find this Martingale and take Katherine by the hand and lead her home.

With any kind of luck.

Chapter Sixteen

"Hibbing Leather Works?" The man pursed his lips in concentration, thought for a moment, then shook his head. "Nope. Sorry."

"They're here in Denver," Arnie persisted.

"Sorry," the man at the pharmacy repeated. "I don't know them." He brightened. "Why don't you look them up in the telephone directory? If they're any kind of an up-to-date outfit they'll have a phone and be listed."

"Sir?" Arnie gasped. But the helpful pharmacist had already turned and was fetching a slim, cardboard-backed gray book off a nearby counter. "Hibbing, you said? Hibbing?" He leafed through the pages, licked a finger, and turned more pages, mumbling, "F . . . G . . . here's H . . . Hancock, Hanratty, Hereford Lumber . . ." He smiled. "Hibbing Leather, here it is right here. The number is eight-four-one-seven. Do you want to use the telephone, son? Right over there. Just tell the operator you want eight-four-one-seven, right?"

Arnie glanced over his shoulder in the direction the man indicated, but all he saw was a large wooden closet sort of thing. Perhaps the telephone was inside it. Or maybe not. Arnie didn't really want to know. Modern ideas were fine, he was sure, but . . . he didn't feel all that modern himself just at that moment. Having to try and figure out a telephone on top of everything else right then was . . . well . . . that would be

64

just a bit too much. "Does it . . . does it give a street address there, sir?"

The pharmacist looked at him for a moment but mercifully said nothing about Arnie's fears. "Corner of Creek and Ellis, son. You go back out onto Colfax here and turn left, then it's, oh, a couple miles out. Let me tell you what to look for. . . ."

Chapter Seventeen

The pharmacist's 'couple' of miles had become something closer to four or five, and it was late in the afternoon by the time Arnie reached the low-roofed, sprawling buildings that made up the Hibbing Leather Works shop. Most of the work-benches were empty, the cutters and hole punchers and waxers and sewers and whatnot having already put their tools away and gone home for the evening.

The inside of the place was mostly empty, but the smell of fresh, clean leather remained. It was an aroma that Arnie loved. If a body had to spend his days indoors working at some set task, this might be one he could put up with, being surrounded by the scent of leather all the day long.

Over close by the windows, Arnie could see a gray-haired man bent over a snake pit of strapping material, separating and sorting the thin strips of tough leather, presumably getting them ready for the next day's work.

Nearer to the front door there were a pair of women at desks. They were checking slips of paper and jotting something from those into large, canvas-bound ledger books.

In a glass front office there was a man in sleeve garters and spectacles poring over another of the big ledgers.

Everyone in view, few though they were, was occupied with his or her work, so Arnie wandered over to the side, where several large photographs were proudly displayed on the wall. They were, he had to admit, impressive.

The first was of a hitch with—he counted—forty-two head of matched horses drawing a dray so polished and gleaming that you knew this was a show-off rig. No freight had ever marred the varnish in the bed of that wagon, no sir. But the hitch—Arnie'd never heard of one bigger than forty horses, which was probably why they'd made up a team of forty-two—was magnificent.

The second showed a gang plow rig on which thirty-six horses—again he'd laboriously counted, tongue firm at the side of his mouth while his finger stabbed at each horse in line—pulled eight sets of plows. Both the plows and the horses were arranged in fans, everything joined in the middle by a single, massive spreader.

The final photo was of a hay stacker, a gigantic incline made of heavy timbers and fed by a huge pushrod powered by, again, an unusually large number of horses. Hay was thrown into the bottom of the ramp, then the horses—hitched behind the pusher—shoved it all the way to the top so that it spilled onto a growing stack that would be thirty feet or more tall when the stack was completely built. Once the push ram reached the top and the hay was dumped onto the stack, the horses then had to back away, still supporting the weight of the pushrod, so the stacker could be reloaded. Arnie never heard of a stacker with more than eight horses on it. It was one thing to drive horses in a pulling hitch, but it was even more difficult to manage them on a stacker in which they had to work walking forward and again backing away.

And this rig . . . he leaned close to the photo and began to count.

"Twenty-four," a voice behind him said.

Arnie turned. The man in sleeve garters had come out of his office and come up behind without Arnie hearing. "Twenty-four? Wow."

"We designed the harness for all those hitches," the man told him proudly. "Designed, fabricated, and even trained the teams to go with them. The plows and stacker we made for a gentleman out east of here. He has what you might call a rather large spread, and he likes to do things on a large scale. The wagon there, that's our own company hitch. We only put up the big hitch for Fourth of July parades and the state fair, special events like that. We have a twenty-four-horse outfit that we send out to ordinary events. But everybody who sees the big hitch remembers Hibbing Leather, I can tell you that.''

"Yes, sir, I'd think they would.''

"Can I help you with something, son? Looking for work? I can always use a another cutter if you have patience enough to be careful and sense enough to follow a pattern.''

"Thank you, sir, but that isn't how you can help me.'' Arnie introduced himself and accepted the gent's offer of a handshake. The man was shop manager, John Drewry by name.

"Pleasure to meet you, sir,'' Arnie said, meaning it. And in truth most of the people he'd come across since leaving home had been pleasant and helpful and kind. That was kind of a nice thing to know. "What I'm doing here, sir, is looking for one of your employees. Fellow called Chance Martingale. Do you happen to know if he's here now? Or where I can find him?''

Drewry pursed his lips. "Martingale?'' He shook his head. "I don't have anyone in the shop by that name. Although it sounds familiar now that I think about it.'' He grunted, then turned. "Mrs. Varham, do we have anyone working here by the name of Martingale? Chance Martingale, was it?'' he added, looking back at Arnie.

The ladies at the desks both looked up in response to the question. The nearer and older of them frowned and said, "No, no one by that name that I can think of.''

"He doesn't work in the shop here,'' Arnie said. "He's a . . . I guess a salesman. Travels through Cheyenne about every month or five weeks. Or so I'm told.''

"We have a man who covers Wyoming and Montana for us,'' the lady said, "but his name is Martin. Claude Martin.''

Arnie grunted. "I bet that'd be him. Do you know where I can find him?''

"Not here, I can tell you that. Those salesmen,'' she sniffed and rolled her eyes but declined to elaborate on the exact, and no doubt disreputable, traits of traveling salesmen.

"Do you happen to have his home address? I . . . it's important. Please?''

Chapter Eighteen

Claude Martin—Chance Martingale almost had to be a fancied-up version of the name, meant to impress gullible young girls—lived on the other side of Denver. Naturally.

After walking all the way out to the harness company from downtown, Arnie's feet hurt. His legs were weary and there were sharp pains in his calves. Hard work was one thing. He could do that from can-see to can't-see and never complain. But he sure wasn't used to this walking stuff. And didn't want to get used to it, either.

Nor did he want to walk all the way back to town and then some in order to find Martin's house. He rode shank's mare just far enough to get back to the trolley tracks, then paid out a five-cent piece so he could sit down and loaf the rest of the way. It was, he figured, worth that.

"This is your stop next, Sonny," the trolley conductor told him, pointing. "Go up that street two blocks and turn left. Up toward the top of that hill. Then it's another, oh, I dunno, another three or four blocks west. Watch the street numbers. You won't have any trouble finding it."

Arnie thanked the man and picked up his saddle and bed. Lordy, but his feet hurt. More so after sitting down, he thought. But he didn't begrudge the trolley ride. Not hardly.

He followed the directions the trolley conductor had given him and repeatedly checked the bit of paper the lady back at the leather company had written Martin's address on, and by and by he stood at the side of a narrow, dusty street, looking across a low picket fence into the yard of a tiny, but quite tidy, little wood frame house.

The place was small but well tended to. Not exactly the sort of thing he would have expected for a scoundrel and ne'er-do-well like this Claude Martin.

There were lilac bushes planted on either side of a front porch—the porch was only six or seven feet across and probably should have been called a stoop rather than a porch except for the fact that it was roofed, with four-by-four timbers for pillars supporting the shingled roof—and a small tree in a front corner of the little bitty yard was propped up with sticks and showed signs of faithful hand-watering as someone struggled to help the immature tree grow and someday prosper.

The house itself was narrow and ran deep on the property, which was only thirty or so feet wide but appeared to run back from the road about a hundred feet, give or take.

The place was painted a bright, clean white. Not whitewash either, but real paint. The difference was obvious. Decorative shutters—they didn't look like they could actually be closed—were beside each of the two front windows. Those were painted too, a sort of slate-blue color that made the little house look extra nice. Looking down along the side of the house, Arnie could see that there were no shutters flanking the few windows there, only on the street side, where they would do the most good toward improving appearances.

There were window boxes under each of the front windows. These were planted with some small puffs of greenery that no doubt would blossom in due course, although at the moment it was impossible for him to tell what kind of flowers they would eventually bear.

In all, the Martin home was modest but pretty. And very nicely kept.

Arnie swallowed hard in an attempt to dislodge the bullfrog that had crawled up into his throat.

Then, gathering his resolve around him like a cloak, he lifted the latch on the front gate and let himself into Claude Martin's yard.

Chapter Nineteen

Arnie didn't know whether to spit or go blind. He'd been prepared to come face-to-face with Claude Martin. Or Chance Martingale, if that was what the kidnapper wanted to be called. He actively wanted to see Katherine.

But . . . who was this small woman in the doorway?

She was tiny, well short of five feet tall, and young. Arnie guessed she was little older than Katherine, even though she had a shy toddler peeping around the side of her skirts and clinging to the hem of her apron. And in addition to that wee one it was plain to see that the girl—woman—was in the family way again. Either that or she was hiding a goose under her dress, for her belly was big enough to overflow a roasting pan, although she was otherwise petite and delicately built.

"I was, um, looking for a, well, a Mr. Martin," Arnie stammered.

The little woman smiled. "Do you work with my husband, Mr. . . . ?" She allowed the matter of the name to trail away suggestively.

"I, um, no ma'am," Arnie said awkwardly. He remembered, much too late, that he still had his hat on and immediately swept it off, setting his saddle down so he could grip the brim with both hands.

"May I tell him who is calling?" she asked, trying once more to satisfy convention.

71

"Yes, ma'am, I, uh, Rasmussen, ma'am, Arnold Rasmussen."

"Of course, Mr. Rasmussen. Please wait here." The woman smiled again—she wasn't really all that pretty as females go, but there was something wholesome and appealing about her that Arnie liked—and she took her infant . . . it was still young enough to be in dresses, and Arnie couldn't tell if the baby was a boy or a girl . . . and went off toward the back of the house, leaving the front door ajar so as not to offend her husband's guest.

Martin—or Martingale—appeared a minute after. He was in shirtsleeves and was carrying a copy of the *Rocky Mountain News*. The fancy man—Arnie liked the SOB even less now than the one time he'd seen him up in Alder Creek—frowned and gave Arnie a looking-over, obviously with no idea who Arnie was or what he wanted here.

"Where's Katherine, damn you?" Arnie blurted.

Martin's frown deepened into a scowl and he shot a glance over his right shoulder. "Don't be so loud, man. Who are . . . oh, now I remember. The hayseed, right? From up in Wyoming. What is this? Are you still angry because I outbid you at the auction?"

"You know what I'm angry about, damn you. You kidnapped Katherine Mulraney. Where is she? What've you done with her?"

Martin looked toward the back of the house again and stepped out onto the tiny front porch. "Come down here so we can talk more freely," he said, taking Arnie by the elbow and guiding him off the porch and across the yard until they were standing beside the picket fence, practically trampling a bed of some sort of flower cuttings.

"It's no wonder you don't want to be overheard," Arnie said. "Be hard on that lady to find out her husband's a kidnapper."

"You know better than that," Martin snapped.

"Like hell I do," Arnie returned, his temper commencing to heat up. "You came at her like a fox in a henhouse and lured her off with lies and false promises and . . . and I don't know what all else. You took her off against her will and—"

"What is your name again, boy?" Martin demanded.

Arnie stuck his chin forward and balled his fists. "My name is Arnold Rasmussen, and I've come here, mister, to get my girl back."

"Your girl, Rasmussen? Your girl? My God, boy, you don't have any idea what you're talking about. And Kate isn't your damn girl. Never was, I'd wager. She damn sure isn't yours now."

"Where—?"

"Let me tell you a few truths, Rasmussen. You won't like them and probably you'll acuse me of lying to you, but what I have to say is the natural truth. I took that girl away with me, sure. But not because I wanted to. All I wanted that day was a little fooling around. You know. Have a bite of sweet to eat and then maybe lift the dumb broad's skirt after. It isn't like that sort of thing is unusual. Happens all the time if a fellow knows what he's doing. It works out short and uncomplicated and no harm done. Not to anybody. Except your Kate, she wouldn't have it that way.

"Oh, she gave me what I wanted, right enough. I didn't even have to work around to it. First thing when she got me alone she grabbed for me and laughed and said she was wanting it. Oh, she's a bold one, your Kate is. Knew right what she was doing, and had plenty of experience too, let me tell you. She knows how to make a man crazy, that one does.

"Then when that first time was over with she gave me this smile like butter wouldn't melt in her mouth and said I was going to have to take her to St. Louis, or maybe San Francisco or Kansas City, to keep her from telling the sheriff up there that I'd taken advantage of her. *Me* take advantage of *her*? I was the one being taken advantage of. That's the truth of it. But she gave me this smug, snide little smile and picked up a handful of hay that she dribbled over her dress and then under her skirt so the grass stems were on her pantaloons. Evidence. She was showing me what kind of evidence she could display to the sheriff if I didn't do what she said.

"The little bitch told me she wanted to go with me. If I took her away from there . . . what's the name of your hick burg? Something-or-other Creek? Sure, Alder Creek, that's it

... she said if I'd take her to the city she'd not say a word to the sheriff about me raping her ... Christ, she was the one making all the moves, damn her ... and she'd give me everything I could handle along the way.''

Martin rubbed the back of his neck and looked around to make sure his wife had not come out onto the porch. He lowered his voice and said, ''That was the one thing she didn't lie about, Rasmussen. That girl like to wore me out between Alder Creek and the time I got her down here to Denver, which she settled for since I couldn't take her to San Francisco or any of those other places. She shrugged and said Denver was big enough to start with. She'd get the rest of the way on her own. And I believe she will. Oh, yes I do. The way that girl can ... well, never mind just exactly what it is that she can do. She can do it mighty well, that's all. Like to wore me out, she did. And I'm a very manly fellow.''

Arnie wanted to punch the lying son of a bitch square in the mouth. But first he needed to know more from him. ''Where ... where is Katherine now?''

''God knows,'' Martin told him. ''She wanted me to take her to where the doxies operate, and that's what I did. I put her into a hack at the train depot and told the driver to take her to Larimer Street. Then I gave the guy a quarter and shut the door. I haven't seen her since and don't want to. I mean, it's one thing to fool around a little when I'm out on the road and lonesome. But I don't foul my own nest, if you see what I mean. I have a nice family here and a good wife and I wouldn't want ... well, I wouldn't want anything that would come along to hurt her. You know?''

''Larimer Street,'' Arnie repeated.

''That's right.''

''But you don't know where on this street she might be?''

Martin shook his head. ''I didn't go with her. Just put her in the hack and then went my own way. I haven't seen her since and don't expect to.''

Arnie thought it over. He was a head and a half taller than Claude Martin—the sometime Chance Martingale—and outweighed the man by probably fifty or sixty pounds. A fancy pip-squeak like Martin who worked—if you could call it that—with lies and figures could never hope to stand up to someone Arnie's size. Not if the sonuvabitch had an ax to defend himself with. It just wouldn't be fair to hit him.

Right! Arnie thought.

And punched Claude Martin in the face just as hard as ever he knew how.

Chapter Twenty

It was well past dark by the time Arnie found his way to the district where Katherine was said to be. By then Arnie's feet hurt worse than ever; his stomach was grumbling and complaining for the lack of supper; he was tired from lugging his saddle and bedroll around all the day long . . . and he was really in fairly good spirits.

Despite Claude Martin's many lies, Arnie had the situation pretty much figured out.

Denials and protests aside, that SOB Martin had somehow forced Katherine to come away with him. It hadn't been at all the way he'd said. Arnie was clear on that point.

Then, afterward, he'd shamed her. That is to say, in order to protect himself from retaliation, Martin had convinced her that Katherine should not go home and face the shame of being seen again among folks who knew her.

That, obviously, was why she hadn't rushed to the nearest telegraph office the minute she was out from under Martin's thumb here on Larimer Street.

That or . . . Arnie's heart practically stopped its beating there in his chest and of a sudden he felt faint; a chilling cold sweat popped out on his forehead and his face twisted in anguish as the ugliness of another possibility struck him. . . . Either it was like Arnie'd been thinking, or possibly, just maybe, Katherine had been sold into a shameful sort of servitude.

Arnie felt fear and frustration well up inside him.

Oh, he'd heard about such things. Everyone had, of course. There were veiled allusions made in magazines like *The Police Gazette* and that ilk. There were sniggering comments and heady whisperings among boys just entering puberty. Arnie knew of such things, more or less, like anyone else was apt to do.

But never had he thought of this—white slavery, that was what they called it—as ever having any particular meaning in the life of anyone he might ever know.

Oh, God! White slavery. It was . . . it seemed incredible that such might be his own sweet Katherine's fate.

White slavery was something that happened in far-off places like San Francisco or decadent places like New Orleans or impossibly foreign places like New York. White slavery surely was not something that could ever touch anyone in Alder Creek, Wyoming.

And yet . . .

If that was what Claude Martin had done to Katherine, Arnie would go back there and find the man and . . . and hurt him. Really and truly hurt him. And . . . and tell his wife about all of it. He swore he would. And . . . and he didn't know what else. But Claude Martin hadn't heard the last of this. Not if it proved that was what he'd gone and done to Katherine.

First, though, the very first thing that had to be done, was that Arnie had to find Katherine.

He would do that if he had to barge into every saloon and dance hall and bawdy house on Larimer Street and look into the face of every girl who worked there and every man who cavorted there.

He would do whatever it took in order to find her and then he would . . . He was not entirely sure what he would do then.

Hold her. Assure her that his affections were unchanged. Remind her that she was the victim of a scoundrel and not the perpetrator of any misdeed.

First of all, though, he had to find her. Then he would worry about gentling her and taking her home again.

Just as soon as he found her.

Chapter Twenty-one

Larimer Street was a disgusting sort of place, wicked and wanton and without any sense of shame or decency.

In truth, though, the sights and sounds and scents of it brought a queasy fluttering of excitement into Arnie's belly, an eagerness, not to participate—of course not—but, well, to *see*. He'd heard about places like this. Now . . .

Denver's district of decadence was half a dozen or so blocks long and two or three wide, taking up a portion not only of Larimer Street itself but of the surrounding blocks as well.

It was a busy, burly hodgepodge of saloons, dance halls, and whorehouses. And even back-alley opium dens, or so Arnie was informed when he inquired about the peculiar, slightly sweetish odors that came from the occasional alley mouth.

Busy? He reckoned so. If downtown Denver was busy during afternoon business hours, then Larimer Street was positively frantic after dark.

Men—there were no women on the sidewalks here—shoved and pushed and bulled their way about in this direction and that, all as determinedly active as so many ants when their hill has been stomped on.

Tinkle-tink piano music, yips of hilarity, and roars of disappointment drifted out of the open doorways along the brightly lighted walkways, the whole district alight with the glow of gas lamps and, more so, the lights streaming out of so many beckoning front windows.

There were even electrified lights in some of the more handsome saloons. Arnie stood for a time staring at those, marveling at that modern wonderment of which he had heard and read although there was no such in little Alder Creek and likely never would be. Electric lights. It was amazing. But certainly not the only thing of interest in the Larimer Street district. The most exotic perhaps, but there was much else to capture the attention. Whether a fellow wanted his interest captured or not, actually.

Barkers stood before the entries of the larger and more prosperous establishments, men who loudly whistled and grabbed at sleeves and invited passing gents inside to: "Have your first beer on the house, friend. Free for nothing, no charge; yes, you heard me right, no charge." "Honest tables here, Mac. Wager a dime and you could win yourself a fortune. Just one dime, Mac, and you could be the big winner tonight, but you'll never know how you'd do if you don't come in and play. That's right, Mac, just tell the dealer you're a pal of mine, see, and he'll treat you square." "Best-looking girls this side o' KC, buddy, guaranteed. Take your pick an' give her a whirl 'round the ol' dance floor, eh? See how she feels afore you do that other dance, eh?" "Free lunch! Nickel beer and the lunch is free. You there. That's right, you. How's about the best free lunch anyplace in Denver?"

The barker's fingers plucked at Arnie's elbow and he repeated his spiel. "Free lunch, son, the best in Denver. Only five cents for the beer and all you can eat. How about it, hey?"

Arnie's stomach churned in response to the thought of food. Five cents for a beer and a lunch spread too? That sure didn't sound bad. He had to eat anyway, didn't he? And a regular supper would cost an awful lot more than a nickel. Arnie smiled and nodded and let the barker draw him toward the waiting doorway.

Chapter Twenty-two

Damn, that was good. Arnie's belly was full and his mood was happy and he couldn't remember feeling that fine in . . . whenever. He reached in front of a fat man wearing vest and shirtsleeves and no proper coat—no class, the man definitely had no class at all—and helped himself to another pickled egg and a crumbling chunk of rat cheese.

"You want another beer there, don't you?" the bartender growled as he watched the food disappear.

"Yeah, sure, one more won't hurt," Arnie said amicably. After all, it was only polite. If you were going to enjoy the lunch free for nothing, then it was only right to buy a couple of beers in return. They'd explained that to him, and he thought it was reasonable.

He'd had . . . was this his third coming now or the fourth? He wasn't real sure. Not that it made any difference. He hadn't had too much or anything. He was fine. Hey, he was better than fine. He was terrific. He felt tall and strong and full of himself. His face had gotten just the wee tiniest bit stiff and his nose was getting numb, but that was all. And there wasn't anything special about that, surely.

The bartender put the fresh beer in front of him—Arnie hadn't realized before this evening just how tasty and refreshing a beer could be—and took away some of the change Arnie'd left on the counter.

"Think I'll have another," Arnie mumbled to no one in particular, and reached for another egg.

"Help yourself," the fat man said. Arnie liked the fat man. He was a nice fellow. Very pleasant company. "Care for an egg?" Arnie offered.

The fat man accepted the egg Arnie handed him and took some boiled ham to munch with it.

"Listen, uh, I gotta . . . you know . . . go out back?"

"What of it?" the fat man asked.

"Would you, um, watch my saddle here while I'm gone?"

The fat man grinned. "What's it do, tricks?" He began to laugh.

That didn't sound so funny to Arnie, but that was all right. The fat man was just trying to be friendly. "Yeah, that's right. It does tricks, so keep an eye on it for me, would you?"

"Be right here when you get back," the fat man assured him.

Arnie thanked the man, several times over, and wandered away from the bar. The floor felt insubstantial underfoot. Like the boards were loose or something. Still, by walking slow and careful, Arnie managed to make his way across the sawdust-strewn floor and out the back door.

The outhouse was supposed to be . . . he wasn't sure where it was supposed to be. Somewhere out back. Wasn't that what the bartender told him a while back? He thought so. So where the heck . . . ah, there was a path. And the glow from a lantern to guide the way. And there, right over there, that would be the outhouse. Good. The pressure in his bladder was close to the limits of comfort and—

"Hey! You don't hafta be in such a hurry," Arnie protested as someone jostled him from behind.

He heard the footsteps and felt the presence and then strong hands had hold of his upper arms. Two men, one on each side. "Hey!" he yelped again.

Neither man said anything. They didn't let go of him either. They turned him around and he saw there was a third man with them.

This guy was big. About as tall as Arnie and with wide, heavy shoulders. He wasn't fat, though, like Arnie's friend back inside the bar. This fellow wasn't the least little bit fat, no sir.

"Whyn't you just—" Arnie didn't have time to finish the sentence. The third man punched him in the stomach, hard, while the first two continued to hold his arms.

Arnie was taken by surprise. He would have braced himself if he'd known the blow was coming, and it wouldn't have hurt so awful bad. As it was, the big fellow's fist buried itself wrist-deep or thereabouts, and drove every scrap of breath clean out of Arnie's lungs.

The man hit him again before Arnie had a chance to holler or kick or do anything, and this time Arnie puked out all the beer and free lunch he'd been so busy stuffing into his belly for the past hour or more.

A stream of hot vomit sprayed out of Arnie's mouth—and a fair amount of it out through his nose as well—and soiled the big fellow's shirt and trousers.

The man shouted some awfully nasty things, and hit Arnie some more.

Arnie pretty much lost track of things after that. Pretty much lost his sense of feeling too, which was more of a blessing than not, as the two who'd been holding him took over from their buddy while the big one gagged at the smell of the stuff that was all over his clothes, and turned away to try and clean himself.

The others weren't so preoccupied though, darn it, and they set in to thumping and kicking and in general pummeling Arnie about as hard and as fast as the two of them were able.

Somewhere in all that, Arnie found himself lying on the footpath, curled into a tight ball to protect himself from the rain of kicks and punches, arms wrapped tight over his head and everything fuzzy and woozy and uncertain. Not only his nose was numb now, but just about every part of him. He could taste the sour puke in his mouth and hear the blows striking him more than feel them any longer, and then pretty soon the whole affair sort of got dim and faded gently away, until Arnie was able to let himself go limp and loose and just sort of drift away into sleep.

The last thing he remembered was hearing the sound of a

voice. He didn't know which of the three was talking. Didn't much care either.

"Go home, boy. Go back to Wyoming where you belong."

Arnie sighed and let go of the last shreds of consciousness.

Chapter Twenty-three

If there was a single muscle, joint, or bone in Arnie's body that failed to hurt, he sure couldn't find the thing. He hurt, quite literally, from one end to the other. From his scalp to the tips of his toes. He hadn't known it was possible to hurt that bad. Even the time that damned old stumble-footed blue roan fell and landed on top of him and busted four of his ribs, Arnie hadn't hurt that bad.

Worse, he couldn't see to figure out what was what. His eyes were glued shut, by dried pus he supposed, and he couldn't pry them open no matter how much he screwed his face or twisted about. Couldn't reach them with his hands either, because those seemed to be held under some sort of restraint. Had the bullyboys who beat on him tied him up afterward? That didn't make any sense. But then none of this was making much in the way of sense to him. Arnie thought about crying some—hey, if nothing else that might loosen the gunk that was sticking his eyes shut and let him see a little—but it had been an awful long time since he'd gone and cried, and he didn't really want to do it again now.

He settled for shooting his jaw this way and that—Lordy, but that did hurt—and trying to snatch his eyelids open that way.

"You can quit that," came a voice to him from somewhere nearby. "Your eyes are swole up so bad you wouldn't be able

84

to see anything out of them anyway, even if you could get them open a little.''

"Who . . . who are you?'' Arnie wasn't sure that it wasn't one of the men who'd beaten him, maybe wanting to come back for more exercise.

"Brad Thomas. Who're you, boy?''

Arnie told him. "Have we . . . have we met, Mr. Thomas?''

"You might as well call me Brad, boy. I mean, Arnie. And I suppose you could say that we've met. You asked me to keep an eye on your things when you went out back the other night. Well, I did. Your saddle and blanket roll are over there in the corner.''

"Corner? Did I hear you to say . . . did you say 'the other night,' sir?''

"I said that, yes.''

"This isn't—?''

"You've been here, mm, this would be the third day.''

"But what—?''

"Don't ask me who did this to you. I don't have any idea. Somebody found you lying on the ground out by the backhouse and they thought we were together, I suppose because we'd been seen talking earlier.''

"You . . . took me in?''

"It was either that or leave you lying there. Which I suppose I might have gone and done except I wouldn't have any use for a saddle.'' There was a lightness in his tone of voice when he said that, and Arnie felt sure the fat man—Brad Thomas, that is—was smiling.

"Thank you, sir. Uh, where . . . ?''

"You're in my room at Mrs. Edith Elroy's boarding house.''

"I've put you out of your own bed?'' Arnie asked.

"Naw. We brought a folding cot up from the cellar. Just sort of stuffed you into a corner and let you be.''

"I've put you to a lot of trouble.''

"Not so much. We've mostly just left you alone. Besides, Mrs. Elroy is used to me dragging broken things in. You know—birds with busted wings and like that. Last year I brought a puppy home. Little bastard got run over by a delivery wagon. Couldn't let it lie there and die in the street, so I brought it home and gave it to Mrs. Elroy's daughter.'' He laughed. "That kept her from throwing it and me both out, you see."

"You gonna give me to the daughter too?" Arnie asked.

"It's a thought, boy. Not that you look worth keeping right now. Whoever robbed you did a right fair job of mussing you up."

"Robbed?" Arnie blurted.

"Of course robbed. What the hell did you think?"

"I didn't—"

"Don't worry about that right now. You don't take up much room, and you sure haven't been eating enough to bother about. Not since you got here. Come to think of it, Mrs. Elroy's been keeping some broth warm for when you got around to coming around. Are you hungry?"

He hadn't been. But now his belly rumbled and the spit began to run in his mouth at the thought of food, even though the last thing he remembered he'd been freshly full up with the free lunch spread back at that saloon. But that had been . . . what was it the fat man had said? . . . three days ago? No wonder he was so hungry.

Arnie tried to lift his hands to his mouth and once again was thwarted. For a moment there he felt panicky and cried out.

"Hey, hold still. You're all right."

"But my hands. I can't raise my hands. What's wrong with my hands?"

"They're tucked under the covers, that's all. Now hold still and don't fret yourself. I'll go downstairs and see if that broth is still hot. I won't be long." Arnie heard movement and the sound of a door being opened, then the parting words, "Don't go away, hear?" The fat man's footsteps receded down a hall-way that had an uncarpeted wooden floor and quickly faded from hearing.

Chapter Twenty-four

Something was bothering Arnie. Well, actually there were a lot of things bothering Arnie, chief among them being the fact that he hurt like hell in every part of his body and another being that he had to pee like a sailor, so much so that there was a sharp pain in the vicinity of his bladder and he was pretty sure if nothing happened soon he would have to let go and wet his bed for the first time since he was old enough to understand what shame was. And that was something he wanted to avoid, so he was hoping the fat man, Mr. Thomas, would hurry back.

Even through and above all that discomfort, though, there was something gnawing at him. Something Brad Thomas said to him. He said Arnie was the victim of a robbery. Well, maybe he had been slugged and mugged, sure. His money was gone from his pockets and therefore he'd been robbed. Anybody could understand that.

But what was nagging at Arnie now was . . . *How had those men known to tell him he should go back home to Wyoming?* And why would they care?

You would think if they once found an easy pigeon—and Arnie had to admit that he'd been awfully easy for them to take—they would want him to stay around so he could be plucked again once he recouped his fortunes.

But not these guys. These three, and they surely did act like they knew what they were doing, these guys warned him to go home.

Whyever had they gone and done a thing like that?

Arnie chewed on that some while he waited for the fat man's return. He also dragged his hands out from under the bedspread and felt his face some.

That was a mistake. There were lumps in places he hadn't known he had places, and the bulges where his eyes were supposed to be were all sticky and wet with some sort of ooze that he was just as happy he couldn't see.

Those guys had really done a job on him, damn them. An awful lot more of one than they'd needed just to accomplish an ordinary, every-night sort of robbery.

Why? Why, dammit?

Arnie couldn't help but wonder if there wasn't more to this than a simple thumping and robbery.

There almost had to be.

Chapter Twenty-five

Footsteps. The fat man was coming back. Thank goodness. Arnie was sure he was gonna bust inside of ten seconds if he didn't get a chamber pot. Either that or he would wet the bed. And likely flood half the house too, judging from the way he felt. He didn't wait around about it. As soon as the footsteps sounded like they were inside the room with him he moaned, "Give me the thunder mug. Quick."

He heard a giggle—a girlish giggle—and felt a flush of embarrassment that probably was turning his cheeks into railroad lanterns and was so acute it made him forget for a couple seconds there just how awfully bad he had to go.

The fat man had said something about the boarding house lady having a daughter. But . . . jeez!

The giggles turned into laughter and the footsteps—how come he hadn't paid any attention before to how light the sounds were compared with those the fat man made when he left the room?—came right smack beside him.

"Look, I, uh, I didn't mean anything that, well . . ." He didn't know what to say and just kind of ran out of words at that point.

The girl laughed again and Arnie felt something cool and smooth and hard pressed into his hands. The porcelain thunder mug. Just what he'd asked for. But . . .

"I'll be back in a couple minutes," the girl said.

She left, and he heard the door close behind her. Thank goodness for that small favor anyhow.

He could still feel the heat in his cheeks as he maneuvered the crockery container under the covers and down where he needed it to be.

"I thought I was gonna die right here in this bed," Arnie said. "Die of purantee mortification."

The fat man laughed, the sound of it belly-deep. "It's all right. Andy thought it was cute, that's all."

"Cute. Huh! And what kind of name is Andy, anyway?"

"Short for Andrea. She's a nice kid. And if it makes any difference, she's the one who has to empty and clean all the thunder mugs in the whole boarding house, each and every day. She's a good worker, Andy is. Good kid too. So don't worry about it. You didn't offend her or give her any education that she didn't already have."

"Even so," Arnie groaned.

"Shut up and open your mouth."

"That doesn't make sense."

"Just do it."

Arnie did as instructed. Whatever Mr. Thomas had brought up with him from the kitchen smelled just about heavenly, and Arnie's mouth was watering from the aroma.

"Open up now. And hold still," the fat man ordered.

The broth tasted even better than it smelled. Chicken, lightly seasoned with something that he couldn't identify, and plenty salty. He liked that. He'd always liked salt, and now he was craving it after being without food for a spell.

"That's good," he said.

"Fine. Now hush." The spoon clinked against Arnie's top teeth but he didn't mind. The important thing was how extra fine the chicken broth tasted. He could feel it bottom out in his belly and spread warmth all through him.

"Can I come in now?" The girl's voice came from not far off.

"Sure. He's decent enough."

Mr. Thomas said that, but Arnie reached down quick to feel the blanket and make sure he was covered. He'd embarrassed himself with this girl enough already for one day. He didn't want another incident.

This time he heard the girl's footsteps—very easily distinguished from Mr. Thomas's now that Arnie knew what he was listening to—and something else too. Light, scratching noises that at first he failed to recognize. Then something small and furry bounded onto the bed beside him, landing partially on his belly and hurting like crazy.

"No!" the girl yelped. Too late. The damage was done. Arnie winced but managed to keep from crying out. "I'm sorry. Did he hurt you?"

"Nah, of course not." Which was a lie, but a polite one. Arnie felt the dog's tongue on the back of his hand and on his wrist. He didn't mind. Really. He'd always liked all sorts of animals. He petted the creature and found that it wasn't hardly big enough to be a full dog. A quarter of one maybe, but not a whole dog.

"He likes you," the girl said.

"Of course he does. I have a way with dogs an' small children."

"If you mean me by that remark, mister . . ."

Arnie could hear the heat in her voice. He laughed. "No such of a thing, miss. I wouldn't fun you. Not right now. I've already done enough for one day where you're concerned."

"Well all right then. Do you want me to finish feeding him, Mr. Thomas? Mama has supper ready to go on the table and if you don't get down there pretty soon there won't be anything left."

"You wouldn't mind, Andy?"

"Oh, not that I'd admit to," the girl said lightly.

Arnie heard some shuffling of feet, and the dog ran up and down the side of his bed. Then it was the girl's voice close to his and the fat man's farther away as Mr. Thomas said, "I leave you in better hands than mine, son," and the girl told him to hush and get on downstairs before the other gentlemen ate it all.

It didn't matter which one of them was wielding the spoon, though. The broth was wonderful regardless, and Arnie felt better for having it.

He wanted to eat a gallon of the stuff, but before he could get through that first bowl he felt himself sliding back into sleep. He put up only a token fight against it and the next thing he knew he woke up alone in the room. He was still hungry, darn it. And he had to pee again.

Chapter Twenty-six

"What do you look like?" It was the middle of the third day after he'd awakened. Mr. Thomas was working—he clerked in a store somewhere—and Andy had brought Arnie's lunch upstairs. She'd also brought along a fresh basin of hot water and Epsom salts to use for soaking his eyes. The girl had pretty much taken over Arnie's care during daytime hours when the fat man was away at his job. She was patient with him, endlessly changing the rags that she used to soak his eyes, and sometimes reading to him. The only novels she seemed to have were romances, sappy and corny and boring, but Arnie would not have complained for anything. He enjoyed the company and the sound of her voice. And he discovered that he kind of liked having the dog curled up against his side while Andy sat in a chair nearby to do her reading. He didn't know what the dog looked like either.

"Are you serious?" Andy asked him.

"Sure I am."

"Well, if you must know . . . this is awfully embarrassing . . . if you absolutely have to know, sir, I'm sixteen years old. I have long yellow hair . . . it's done up in a proper bun now, of course . . . and there are those who—did I mention to you that this is embarrassing?—there have been people . . . boys . . . or . . . well, or men too . . . who say I am . . ."

She hesitated so long that Arnie broke the silence for her. "Pretty?" he asked.

"I've been called that, yes."

"I kind of thought so," Arnie admitted. "You sound pretty."

"Is that supposed to be a compliment?"

"If you like."

"Let me think on it. I'll let you know later. Are you hungry? Never mind, you don't have to tell me. You're always hungry, aren't you?"

"I'm being a nuisance, aren't I? Is your mother complaining about me? I don't have . . . look, I mean this now, I want you to keep a record of whatever my room and board should be and I'll find a way, sometime, to pay her back. I promise I will."

He felt Andy's hand on his wrist. "Don't get so worried about everything. I didn't mean . . . well, I didn't mean *that*. You know? And Mama hasn't said a word of complaint about you. Truly she hasn't. I apologize for not making myself clear. I was just, um, being playful. That is a very bad habit, isn't it? I really must learn to grow up and act serious."

"No, you're fine, I just—"

"Be quiet now. Here's your lunch." Arnie felt her lift the dog down off the bed and then she propped some extra pillows behind his back so he could sit in an almost upright position while he ate. He had improved to the point where he could feed himself now. Andy made sure everything was cut up into small pieces, and she gave him a bowl and spoon rather than a plate and fork to eat with. But he could manage those on his own. That had felt a considerable accomplishment.

"You still can't see anything?" she asked.

"I can make out whether it's light outside better now than I could. I can't see any shapes or anything like that, but I think the swelling is going down now. Soon, I think. Real soon."

"I'm going to miss sitting here with you and Buttons, reading to you and like that." She giggled. "If nothing else, it keeps me from having to do other work around the house."

"I'll never be able to repay you for all you've—"

"Hush!" she snapped, her voice stern. Arnie had noticed before that she did not seem comfortable with thanks. "I have to go back down now and clean up the kitchen. Mama will want to start cooking supper soon, and it's always easier on her if I have things ready."

"Sure." He felt like he'd chased her off, although he couldn't see much of a reason for it.

"When you're done eating, set the bowl down on the bed. I'll be back up to collect it later."

"Yeah, thanks." He heard the girl leave, but the dog stayed behind. When she was well down the hall, Buttons jumped back onto the bed beside him and sniffed at the bowl Arnie was holding. "Settle down, you. I'll give you a bite if there's anything here I don't like. Is that fair, or what?"

The dog didn't answer. And there was nothing in the bowl that Arnie wasn't interested in. Mrs. Elroy was an almighty fine cook, he had to say that about her.

Chapter Twenty-seven

"Don't be so impatient now. Hold still and let me wipe this
. . . there, that seems to be doing the trick. Don't try to open
them just yet. Give me a minute, please." He heard the squish
and drip of water as the girl soaked the rag once more in a
bowl of warm water, then felt the soothing touch of the cloth
on his eyes. The swelling had gone down considerably over
the past couple of days, and now Andy was wiping the gooey
ooze away.

"Don't be surprised if you can't see very well at first," she
said. "I have the curtains pulled, so the room is kind of dark."

Arnie nodded. The girl gently wiped his eyes again and then
took the cloth away. "Try it now."

He had to exert some force to make his eyelids separate.
Then they popped open and he could see. Dimly, the images
fuzzy to begin with. But he could see.

He looked at the girl. And laughed.

Andy. Sixteen, blond, and beautiful. Right. She was a
skinny, freckled, gap-toothed kid of twelve or thirteen. She
giggled and clapped her hands. "You believed me, didn't
you?"

Arnie laughed again.

"You aren't mad at me?"

He shook his head, then patted the side of the bed as he'd
become accustomed to doing over the past few days. A sleek
little white and black rat terrier, hardly bigger than a rat, never

96

GET YOUR 4 FREE BOOKS NOW— A VALUE BETWEEN $16 AND $20

Mail the Free Book Certificate Today!

FREE BOOKS CERTIFICATE!

YES! I want to subscribe to the Leisure Western Book Club. Please send my 4 FREE BOOKS. Then, each month, I'll receive the four newest Leisure Western Selections to preview FREE for 10 days. If I decide to keep them, I will pay the Special Members Only discounted price of just $3.36 each, a total of $13.44. This saves me between $3 and $6 off the bookstore price. There are no shipping, handling or other charges. There is no minimum number of books I must buy and I may cancel the program at any time. In any case, the 4 FREE BOOKS are mine to keep—at a value of between $17 and $20! Offer valid only in the USA.

Name_____

Address_____

City_____ State_____

Zip_____ Phone_____

Biggest Savings Offer!

For those of you who would like to pay us in advance by check or credit card—we've got an even bigger savings in mind. Interested? Check here. ☐

If under 18, parent or guardian must sign.
Terms, prices and conditions subject to change. Subscription subject to acceptance. Leisure Books reserves the right to reject any order or cancel any subscription.

GET FOUR BOOKS TOTALLY
FREE—A VALUE BETWEEN
$16 AND $20

▼ Tear here and mail your FREE book card today! ▼

PLEASE RUSH
MY FOUR FREE
BOOKS TO ME
RIGHT AWAY!

Leisure Western Book Club
P.O. Box 6613
Edison, NJ 08818-6613

AFFIX
STAMP
HERE

mind the terrier, jumped onto the bed at his side.

"Neither one of you is exactly what I expected," he said.

"You really aren't mad at me?"

"Naw, of course not."

"Good. Stay here now. I'll go get your lunch."

The truth, Arnie discovered now that he thought about it, was that he was actually more comfortable about talking with the girl now that he knew she was just a kid. It wasn't like he'd considered himself unfaithful to be talking with Andy when he thought she might be closer to Katherine's age and prettiness. Exactly. But he supposed it had something to do with that. Anyway, there was no wavering in his devotion to Katherine. Nor any lessening of his resolve to find and to rescue her.

It was just . . . well, it was just all right with him to discover that his devoted nurse of these past days wasn't but a gawky child.

That seemed just fine.

Chapter Twenty-eight

"Isn't it a little soon to be venturing outside for your first time, son? You've been awfully weak, you know. Why don't you give yourself more time before you try walking any distance?"

"Thank you, sir, but I have to find Katherine. And those men who beat me up. They weren't just robbing me, you know. They knew who I was and where I was from. What they done to me was deliberate. I need to find out who put them up to it and why. It has to do with my Katherine, Mr. Thomas. I'm sure of it."

"Arnie, you aren't near strong enough to defend yourself if you do find them. You can't take the chance that—"

"Sir, I'm plenty strong and bigger than any one of them. That last time they took me by surprise. And there was the three of them. If I can get ahold of one by himself I'll find out everything I need to know."

"Arnie, I don't think—"

"Please, sir."

The fat man shrugged. "You know your own mind, son."

"Yes, sir. Thank you, sir."

"Are you going back to that same saloon?"

"Yes, sir."

"Would you like me to come along with you?"

"No, sir, though I thank you for the offer. I'll manage this on my own, thanks."

"You should at least have a dollar to spend while you're waiting for one of them to show up."

Arnie hadn't thought of that, but he supposed Mr. Thomas was right. He would not be welcome hanging around the saloon if he could not afford a beer to justify his being there.

"Here." Mr. Thomas dug into his pocket and came up with some change that he handed to Arnie without bothering to count.

"You've been awfully kind, sir. You and the ladies here at the boarding house. I don't know what I'd've done without your help. Or what I'd be able to do without it now."

"That's all right, son. It's the right thing to do. And one of these days you can pass the favor along to someone else. That's all I ask."

"Thank you, sir."

"Well, go on then if you feel you have to. Don't wake me when you come in, hear?"

Arnie grinned. "Yes, sir. Thanks." He picked up his hat and let himself out of the small room he shared with his benefactor.

With any kind of luck tonight . . . he was thinking as he made his way downstairs—his legs weaker and more wobbly than he'd thought after the days of illness and inactivity—and out the front door.

Now if he could just figure out where the saloon district was from here . . .

Chapter Twenty-nine

He found the same bar where he'd been that time before. It wasn't difficult, a few questions of helpful strangers, a ten-minute trolley ride, and there he was. Arnie did feel a certain small chill of trepidation when he walked into the saloon, but that lasted only a moment. Then he was surrounded by the pleasantly mingled odors of beer and sweat and pickling spices as he found a place beside the free lunch and paid for a beer.

The beer was a bright clean flavor on his tongue, crisp and very faintly bitter. He liked it. The ham on the free lunch tray was dried out and tough, but the pickled eggs were as good as he remembered them, and the crackers were fresh and tasty. Arnie quickly ate his fill, then bought a second beer and carried it into a far corner where he would not be so conspicuous. Mr. Thomas hadn't given him all that much change, and Arnie still had to make it through the evening and then pay for a trolley ride back to Mrs. Elroy's boarding house.

He nursed the second beer as long as he reasonably could and was thinking he might have to break down and buy a third when his vigil bore fruit. A man with an all too familiar face came down the staircase from the second story, where a number of individual room doors were visible beyond a railed balcony. Men occasionally left the bar portion of the saloon and made their way up to the rooms. They only stayed in the rooms for brief periods though, ten minutes to a half hour or so, leading Arnie to conclude that the rooms did not serve as an inn but probably hid high-stakes gaming or something on that order, even though poker and faro games were conspicuous in the back part of the saloon floor. The games upstairs, he figured, must be exciting indeed.

Right now, though, his interest lay in the man coming down those stairs. It was one of the men who'd beaten him half to death the last time he was here. Arnie had seen that face, and the other two as well, in his memory practically every time he closed his eyes—well, figuratively speaking, since they'd been glued shut most of that time—since.

This was one of them. Arnie was positive about that. And with any kind of luck . . .

He had the luck. The big man—big but not as much so as Arnie himself—nodded and said something to the bartender that Arnie couldn't hear, then headed out the back door in the direction of the outhouse.

Arnie knew how the deal worked. For sure he did. After all, he'd been jumped himself under similar circumstances. This was his chance to repay the favor. He drained off the last swallow of lukewarm beer, a habit drilled into him over the years by frugal parents of never, ever wasting anything, and set the mug aside, then rose and swiftly followed the hard-fisted brawler out into the young night.

This time, by golly, things were fixing to be different.

Chapter Thirty

The guy came out of the crapper hitching his pants up and finishing buttoning and buckling. He obviously didn't suspect a thing and likely never noticed Arnie standing there in the shadows just about the same place the three plug-uglies had laid in wait for him that time. Oh, this was gonna be just fine.

Arnie let the fellow come too close to get away, then stepped out into the path directly in front of him. "Remember me?"

Surprisingly, the big man didn't seem the least bit unnerved to be confronted like this. In fact, he stopped, smiled, and nodded. "Sure do, young fella. I remember you real well. If I do say so you healed up right nice after the pounding you took. Sorry you didn't take our advice, though, and go back to . . . where was it you come from?"

"Wyoming," Arnie said without thinking about it. After all, dang it, he hadn't come here to have a chat with this guy.

"That's right, I remember now. Wyoming. Nice place, Wyoming. Big. A man could lose himself up there if he was a mind to."

"Losing myself, nor going home neither, isn't what I had in mind," Arnie told him.

"Now let me guess. You come back here because you're mad me and my buddies whipped you and you want to get

102

some back. So you thought you'd catch one of us alone and see if the odds didn't work out better for you.''

"How'd you know that?"

"Sonny, it ain't like it hasn't happened before. And like them other fellows before, I'll tell you what I always do when somebody wants to get back at me. Tonight I ain't being paid to put a hurting on you, so if it's all the same to you I'd as soon leave this thing be. I don't wanta hurt you again and I won't unless you insist on it. But I won't stand here and let you hurt me none either. You see what I'm telling you, son?"

"I see all right, but I can't say it makes me feel any different.''

The big man shrugged. "You got to admit that I tried. Later on, son, I want you to remember that and not come back at me again. I did try. And I'll promise not to do you too bad tonight since I do understand what you're trying to do here. It's a matter of standing up and being a man. Hell, I understand that. So I won't do any worse than, say, break one arm and some ribs. All right?''

Arnie had to give credit where it was due. This fellow wasn't scared. Not a lick of it, even though Arnie stood a good three inches taller than him and likely outweighed him by twenty pounds or so of solid muscle.

"If you think you're able," Arnie said.

"What's your name, son?"

"Arnold Rasmussen. Arnie."

"Nice to know you, Arnie." The big man grinned. "Well, sort of. I still wish you'd change your mind.''

"No, sir, I reckon not."

"Colin."

"Pardon me?"

"My name. It's Colin. If you ever come back . . . I'd be happy to buy you a beer if you come peaceable some time. . . . Ask at the bar for Colin. I'm near always around.''

"Yes, sir."

"Colin," the big man corrected.

"Right. Colin.''

"Look, d'you wanta drop this and go inside? I'll stand treat for the beer if you do."

"No, this is something I expect I got to do."

"Then let's get us to it, Arnold Rasmussen from Wyoming." Colin grinned again and lifted his fists, setting himself but waiting for Arnie to make the first move.

Chapter Thirty-one

Arnie balled his fists tight and jumped. Hard and fast. He swarmed all over Colin the brawler, punching and grunting and throwing a barrage of lefts and rights and still more rights.

It took him a few seconds to realize that he was throwing plenty of punches but he wasn't feeling much of anything on the other end of them. He was throwing but he wasn't hitting. Colin, on the other hand . . .

Arnie felt the first few raps. Then awfully quick his face turned numb and he more heard the thunder of Colin's blows than felt them.

They snapped out of nowhere, jolted him down to his toes and went back to wherever they came from without his hardly ever having a chance to see them coming.

Arnie hunched his shoulders, lowered his head like a bull getting ready to charge, and plunged forward again.

Something—he never saw what—tripped him up and he went sprawling into the gravel of the outhouse path. He'd been there before, he remembered, and that memory drove him back onto his feet, practically as quick as he went down.

He sent a wild, looping right hand out as he lurched upright, and was rewarded with the knowledge that his punch landed flush in Colin's belly and sank in wrist-deep or beyond.

Colin gasped and staggered backward. Arnie wasn't all that experienced when it came to fighting, but he wasn't stupid either. This was his chance and he darn well intended to take it. He stayed low and followed Colin as the big man back-pedaled.

Arnie rained one punch after another into Colin's breadbasket, not giving him time to recover his breath. The tactic was working, and for a change it was Arnie who had the upper hand. He didn't intend to lose it either. He stayed squarely in front of the reeling, gasping Colin, continuing to pound Colin's gut and sternum. He heard something that might have been a rib going, and knew if he could just keep this up a little longer . . .

A bomb burst just inside his left temple, and Arnie felt his knees sag.

That blow was followed by another that smacked into his jaw and whipped his head around. He staggered, but hit Colin again.

Colin went down, dropping onto his butt and then flopping over onto his back. He looked plenty ready to call it quits for the night.

Arnie started to smile. Then winced as a sledgehammer blow landed in his short ribs on the left side of his aching body. For several painful moments he stood there trying to comprehend this new pain. Then, groggy and barely able to stand, he looked to his left.

The other one—Karl, Colin had called his partner—was there. Looking unruffled and mean as hell.

"What the . . . ?"

"Sorry, kid. Colin saw you when he first come downstairs a while ago. He had the barkeep get word to me to back him up. Just in case. I wouldn't 've done anything here . . . I want you to know that, see . . . except I can't let my pard get busted up by your lucky break. You see what I'm telling you, Arnie?"

"You know my name?"

"I been standing right behind you, listening in, practically since you come outside. I heard you and Colin talking. And since he promised he wouldn't do more than one arm and a couple ribs, I won't take it past that neither. All right?"

"Dammit, you aren't being fair," Arnie protested.

"Son, me and Colin do this for pay. And we ain't paid to be fair."

"But—"

"We won't do you any worse than we have to. Honest. Now come away and do whatever you're a mind to, because I wanta get this over with so I can take care of my pard."

"No, I—" But it didn't matter what Arnie wanted to say. Karl wasn't listening. Colin's partner raised his fists into an awkward-looking guard and moved in with an expression of grim determination.

Arnie hated it, but he couldn't help himself. He felt a cold thrill of absolute fear as—mesmerized like a jacklighted doe— he stood and watched Karl move in with every intent of doing some serious bodily harm.

Chapter Thirty-two

It wasn't good and it was fixing to get worse. Karl chose his shots with cold, deliberate care, and began the process of disassembling Arnie Rasmussen.

He avoided the face, at least while it was early in the brawler's game, perhaps to make sure Arnie could feel it all as it was happening, with no wooziness to deaden the pain, and bombarded Arnie's liver and kidneys and ribs with hard, calculated blows.

Arnie, a sense of shame nagging at him even while it was happening, virtually stood still and let Karl pummel him while scarcely fighting back.

Oh, he threw a wild, windmilling punch now and then. But he did so in desperation and with no real expectation that he would actually hit, or hurt, the professional bone-breaker. Nor for that matter did he. Arnie's few harried swings sailed and looped and soared all around the big man without once doing him any damage.

And Karl . . . it was bad and only getting worse.

Arnie absorbed a combination of rights, lefts, and more rights to the pit of his stomach, and he doubled over from pain and a lack of wind.

Karl said something that Arnie did not hear and immediately after there was the sharp, whipcrack report of hard fists smacking sharply onto living flesh. *Thwack, thwack, thwack.*

And again. Louder.

Arnie winced and reeled backward. He had taken two, maybe three steps back before he realized he was already so battered that he'd lost feeling even without being punched in the head. How else to explain how he could hear those blows but feel nothing. Absolutely nothing. Not the first small hint of sensation.

Nor was the hitting done with. He heard the sounds again, and once again they came in a set of three. *Thwack, thwack, thump.* This time the sounds were followed by a grunt of pain.

Arnie blinked. And straightened upright.

He squinted, trying to see, to comprehend.

Karl was there in front of him all right. But a good ten feet away by now and reeling backward from a furious onslaught delivered by a short, fat man who—

"Mr. Thomas!" Arnie blurted.

This was most definitely *not* the Bradley Thomas who Arnie knew as his gentle benefactor and roommate.

This gentleman, fat and all, was a dynamo of energy and raw aggression.

This gentleman bounced and bounded, moving lightly on the balls of his feet, bobbing underneath Karl's few wild swings—blows as wild and hopeless, Arnie saw, as his own had been only moments earlier—darting inside Karl's reach to deliver a stinging combination onto Karl's face, or ducking low to whip solid, crunching punishment to the far bigger man's breadbasket.

This gentleman, never mind that he looked so much like Arnie's fat friend Mr. Thomas, overmatched the professional bullyboy Karl as completely as Karl overmatched Arnie.

Incredibly, Mr. Thomas was punching so fast that Arnie had difficulty seeing his hands move. It was as if his punches came out of nowhere to suddenly explode in place. Time after time after time.

Already Karl's face was masked in blood. His nose and lips were split open and pouring the stuff. Arnie watched while with deliberate intent Mr. Thomas rained blows onto the shelf of Karl's forehead, opening his eyebrows with an almost surgical neatness and draining still more blood into the big man's eyes.

Blinded now, Karl staggered and flailed wildly at the night air while Mr. Thomas ducked left and right and left again, moving back and forward, ripping hard blows into Karl's belly and sternum each time he came near, then darting back out of reach of the desperate swings Karl was taking.

Mr. Thomas—Arnie could hardly believe it although he was seeing it with his own wide-open eyes—seemed unruffled. He still had his derby perched undisturbed atop his head, and the tail of his shirt remained inside his trousers. Oh, the cloth was puffed out a little between his waistband and vest. But he did not look like a man who'd been in a fistfight. Not now nor ever his whole life long.

Karl on the other hand . . .

Mr. Thomas took his time about picking the perfect opportunity, then took careful aim and delivered a devastating blow onto Karl's jaw, snapping his head around so hard Arnie was surprised it did not break the big man's neck. Karl's eyes rolled back in his head, and he crashed face forward onto the graveled path to the outhouse. That was a feeling Arnie knew too. And one he did not much care for.

Mr. Thomas turned to Arnie and smiled. "Come along, son. Let's us be getting out of here before these two get their wits about them and decide to fight some more."

The fat man grabbed Arnie by the elbow and pulled, drawing Arnie with him toward the street and safety.

Arnie went along without protest. After all, he knew excellent advice when he heard it.

Chapter Thirty-three

Mr. Thomas grabbed Arnie by the arm and practically threw him into the trolley. He shoved Arnie onto a seat bench and turned to look behind them. By this time, Mr. Thomas was puffing and gasping, gulping for air like a trout on a creekbank.

"It's a good . . . thing that fellow . . . didn't stay up . . . any longer or I'd've . . . passed out my own self." Mr. Thomas grinned and poked Arnie on the shoulder. "But I haven't . . . lost it yet . . . not all . . . of it."

It. Mr. Thomas had *it*, all right. Lordy, Arnie reckoned he did.

"Mr. Thomas."

"Mm?"

"You were . . . how came you to be there tonight?"

"Son, I knew where you were . . . going." He gasped a little more but his breath seemed to be coming a little easier now, and Arnie could see that the fat man's chest was no longer heaving so heavily. "I thought you might need help, so I followed along behind to keep an eye on you. Just in case."

"In case I did exactly what I did do, is that it?"

"Well yes, actually."

"Mr. Thomas, I mean, if you don't mind me asking, well . . . uh, how'd you do what you did back there? That is t'say . . ."

Mr. Thomas grinned again. And held up a finger for Arnie to wait a moment.

The trolley conductor made his way to the back of the car and Mr. Thomas fished in his pocket for change to buy their passage, then took a few extra moments to tuck his shirttail in and straighten a hat that was already straight on his head. He touched the knot of his tie to assure himself that it was in place, then leaned back in his seat and took in a few slow but much easier breaths before he answered Arnie's entirely obvious questions.

With a wink and a laugh he explained, "I wasn't always like this, y'know." He pointed to his more than ample belly and shrugged. "Time was, I was in fine shape. Better than I looked, in fact." He laughed again.

"When I was younger, Arnold, I didn't look near as hard nor near as old as I was. Why, until I was in my late twenties I could pass for fifteen. And did. And I was lean but quick, and a helluva lot stronger than I appeared to be.

"Most of all, you see, I knew what I was doing. I'd been taught the sweet science of gentlemanly fisticuffs, you see, and I traveled with a medicine show and took on local rubes in prizefights."

"You? You were a real prizefighter?"

The fat man laughed. "I know, it seems incredible, doesn't it? But it's true enough. Made a good living at it too, I don't mind telling you. I learned to fight . . . the real thing, I mean . . . when I was a boy not yet needing to shave. We had a neighbor who'd been in the ring himself, and he started teaching me. Then when I left home and hooked up with the medicine show, the 'doctor' taught me the refinements of the game. I was a good learner. And like I said, I was fitter and stronger than I looked to be. I almost never lost a bout.

"The deal was, the barker would bring me out and parade me around and I'd look all innocent and easy, and they'd announce that I was there to take on all comers. Anyone wanting in the ring with me put up five dollars for the privilege against a prize of fifty dollars in gold coin if he could lick me. And never mind how big the rube was. We fought bareknuckle style, a round lasting until one man was off his feet and a timed minute between rounds. The first man to not be able to toe the mark in the center of the ring after the minute was up was the loser.'' Mr. Thomas smiled, remembering. ''Five dollars, and I got two of them to keep. And Doc took care of all my needs the whole time . . . food, a cot in the back of one of the wagons, even bought my clothes for me . . . so I didn't have anything to spend my money on but myself and whatever I fancied. Some days, Arnie, I'd make as much as twenty dollars. In one single day, mind you. My record take was twenty-eight, but that was hard. I was worn out that day even worse than I am right now, let me tell you. But it was grand while it lasted. It surely was.''

''Why'd you quit it if you liked it so much?''

''It's more a matter of it quitting me, son. I told you we fought bare-knuckle. That chops up a man's hands. No matter how you try to protect them, the hands start to go eventually. That's what happened to me. My hands gave out, and I had to get out of the ring. I stayed with the wagons for a while, selling medicines and giving spiels, but my heart wasn't in that stuff. And of course I kept on eating like I always had, except I wasn't in training any more and wasn't fighting, so I began to put on a belly. I'd never had one before then, and it didn't look so good for a fat man to be touting elixirs that were supposed to guarantee instant health. So eventually Doc told me I either had to quit diving so deep into the groceries or leave the outfit. That was right here in Denver sixteen . . . no, it's more like seventeen now, I think . . . years ago. I didn't have anywhere better to be, so I've stayed here ever since.''

Mr. Thomas threw his head back and laughed loud and long. ''I still haven't lost it, have I, Arnie? Not all of it, I haven't.''

''No, sir,'' Arnie agreed happily. ''You sure haven't.''

Chapter Thirty-four

Arnie didn't really need the lap robe. It was almighty hot underneath the darn thing. But the girl seemed at her happiest when she was fussing and arranging and taking care like a mother hen herding her chicks, and so Arnie let Andy have her way about stuff like the robe and the soups and soft foods—it was his insides that were hurting, not his jaw or teeth this time, and he could see just fine thanks to Mr. Thomas keeping Karl from doing any worse damage—but he drew the line at letting her keep him nailed down in the bed. He sat in a wicker chair that she'd dragged in from another room in the boarding house along with an ottoman to prop his feet on. He couldn't complain about the treatment. Even if there was a bit more care offered than he really wanted.

"Can I ask you something?" the girl asked, her eyes wandering around the room everywhere but in Arnie's direction.

He petted the dog that was half asleep in his lap and scratched it behind the ears before he answered. "Sure you can. You or your mother or Mr. Thomas, you can ask me anything you please. I owe you, all three of you."

Andy blushed, but still didn't look at him. She seemed intent on giving her fingernails—her nails were bitten short, he saw, and her fingers chapped—an extra-close examination. "You don't owe us anything."

Arnie shrugged. He supposed it didn't really matter that she missed seeing the gesture.

"That girl . . ." Andy ventured.

"Katherine," he said.

"Yes. Her."

"What about her?"

"Are you going to go on looking for her?"

"Of course I am. That's the reason I came here, you know. To save her from that man."

"But she isn't with him any more. She hasn't been for a long time."

"That doesn't matter. She still needs me."

"You know what she's been doing ever since she left him."

"Since he threw her to the wolves, you mean."

"Yes. Whatever."

"As a matter of fact," Arnie said, "I *don't* know what Katherine has been doing these past couple weeks. None of us knows. Not really. And I don't intend to ask about that when I see her. It isn't . . . it isn't important. The important thing is to save her and make her see that she isn't at fault. No matter what she's had to do lately, it isn't her fault. She's been forced into . . . well, whatever. I don't want to know. I just want to make things right for her. That's what I came here to do, and I won't go back and face her folks, or mine, until I've done what's needed."

"Will you marry her?"

"Yes. I will."

"Even if—?"

"Don't say it, all right? None of that stuff matters."

"You'll keep on looking for her?"

"I said that already."

"Don't you realize if you go back to that part of town to look for her you'll likely run into those men again? You'll have to fight them again."

"I've thought about that," Arnie said. "As soon as I can move around again without feeling like I'm about to fall into two pieces, I'm going to ask Mr. Thomas to teach me about fighting. Doing it the right way, I mean. That way I'll be able to take care of myself if they come at me again."

"You could get hurt, Arnie. You could even get killed. Things like that happen, you know. You don't see it in the newspapers, but you hear things. That part of the city, it isn't safe.''

"I have to find her, Andy. I have to."

The girl sighed and picked a speck of imaginary lint off her apron. "If I read this in a story I think it probably would sound romantic and wonderful. But in real life, Arnie, I think you're being awfully stupid."

She did not wait for him to respond. She stood and gathered her skirts and hurried out of Arnie's convalescent room. Buttons gave Arnie's hand a nudge, and when he did not immediately move to continue scratching him, Buttons scrambled off his lap and, toenails noisy on the polished hardwood flooring, hurried after his mistress.

Chapter Thirty-five

Arnie grunted with the effort of throwing the punch. He threw it just as hard and fast as he knew how. And he meant it to land. It hadn't been like that to begin with. He'd thrown his punches soft and slow to start. Then harder. And harder. And now he was giving it absolutely everything he had. Yet, dammit, just like every time before, he hit . . . nothing. Not a lousy thing.

Mr. Thomas, his fat face red not from effort but from laughing so damn much, just . . . wasn't there when Arnie's fist arrived at the spot where Mr. Thomas's face had been just moments earlier. That or else one of Mr. Thomas's forearms moved, not particularly far nor particularly fast, at least to outward appearances, and somehow that movement was just enough to deflect Arnie's blows scant fractions of an inch past Mr. Thomas's ruddy cheek or laughing mouth.

It was frustrating. Aggravating. The next closest thing to maddening. And there didn't seem to be a stinking thing Arnie could do to make it different. No matter how hard he tried, he just plain could not hit the seemingly easy target Mr. Thomas hung out there in front of him.

Arnie drew back and tried again, hitting out so hard and fast that the force of the blow whistling cleanly past Mr. Thomas's ear was enough to pull Arnie off balance and send him stumbling into Mr. Thomas's chest. Which was the only time so far he'd managed to make any contact with the fat man whatsoever.

"Dammit!" Arnie complained.

Mr. Thomas laughed again and told him, "Don't be upset. Now you can see what I've been trying to explain to you."

"But if I can't ever learn to hit anybody—"

"Try and learn what I teach you, son. It will all come together by and by. And right now what I want is for you to learn to not be hit by the other fellow. After all, if he can't hit you, he can't hurt you. Once you know that, you can worry about what you're going to do to him."

"Yes, sir. If you say so."

"I do. Now pay attention. We're going to do this in slow motion, and this time I'm going to send one at your mug, right? No, put your hands up like I showed you. There, that's better. Now . . . slow . . . slow . . . we're not in any hurry. Use your wrists and the backs of your forearms just like I showed you. That's it. That's right. Now this time a little faster, see . . ."

It was a Sunday afternoon and Mr. Thomas had the day off from work. Arnie's belly was full of the chicken and dumplings—much more in the way of dumplings than chicken, of course, but you had to expect that in a boarding house—that Mrs. Elroy always made for Sunday dinner, and a little while ago it had seemed a fine day to commence Arnie's education in the fine art of fisticuffs. Now, with Mr. Thomas making an idiot of him and half a dozen boarders sitting on the back stoop watching the humiliation of Arnold Rasmussen, he wasn't sure it was such a jim-dandy idea after all.

Too late to back out now, of course.

"Put them up again, son. You're doing fine, really." Mr. Thomas gave him a smile that Arnie supposed was intended for encouragement. "Let's do it again now. A little faster this time. Ready? All right."

The phony punch was delivered at an insultingly slow speed, and Arnie dutifully pushed it aside with the back of his left wrist. Deflect a right hand with the left; block a left with the right; step back from a hook; move into and smother the low ones. Wasn't that what Mr. Thomas had been saying?

Arnie shook his head. He would never get the hang of all this. Never. He was sure of it. Never.

"Good, real good. Now again. Slow again, nice and slow. We've time to speed it up later, son. Once it's all become second nature to you, like."

The fat man smiled and nodded, and Arnie was conscious of the creaking spring and wood-slap of the kitchen screen door opening and closing, and Andy was there sitting among the boarders with Buttons in her lap, and all the men were saying something and laughing, no doubt telling her how silly and stupid and clumsy the big cowboy was and how their fat old Mr. Thomas was making a fool of him.

Still, there wasn't any way Arnie could think of to get out of it now.

And he did want to learn the things Mr. Thomas could teach him. He really did. He just hadn't thought the lessons would be so damned embarrassingly *public*, that was all.

"Right. You're doing good, son," Mr. Thomas kept telling him through the smiles. "You're doing fine."

Chapter Thirty-six

Arnie sighed and pushed back away from the table. It was Thursday evening and he felt pretty good. His belly was full—supper had been pinto beans and rice with chunks of fatty ham swimming in the juice and plenty of vinegar and hot pepper sauce to spice the mixture up if a body liked—and he felt rested and really pretty good again despite the pummeling he'd gotten from the bullyboy named Karl only a few days earlier. There would be no dessert. Mrs. Elroy only fed her people desserts on Sunday and Wednesday evenings.

"All done?" Mr. Thomas asked from the other side of the table.

"Yes, sir."

"Come along then. I have something for you." The fat man pushed away from the remains of his meal and, groaning softly under his breath, stood.

Arnie glanced outside. Mr. Thomas surely couldn't be suggesting another lesson in the yard. It was full dark. The lamps had been lighted almost an hour ago and there was no way they could see well enough outdoors to spar in the slowest of motions. And wouldn't Mrs. Elroy shriek if they tried to do it indoors?

"Not that," Mr. Thomas said, correctly interpreting Arnie's skeptical look. "Come with me."

"Are we going far?"

"Just out to the porch." The front porch, with its ragtag

collection of unmatched rocking chairs and gliders, was the customary after-supper haunt of the boarders.

"Then I won't need my hat."

"No." Even so, Mr. Thomas veered aside rather than going straight on to the vestibule. He went to the row of hooks where the gentlemen were expected to leave their hats and coats and, in inclement weather, their overshoes. "Wait there. You'll see."

Arnie waited while Mr. Thomas dug into his coat pockets for a small package that he withdrew and carried out onto the porch with him. Arnie trailed along behind.

"Down there," Mr. Thomas said, nodding. Without making too obvious a point of it, he took Arnie away from the rest of the boarders, most of whom were busy watching Earl Deimer and Mr. Saccarelli engage in a silent but nonetheless heated chess match. "Have a seat."

Arnie dropped onto a glider and Mr. Thomas sat beside him.

"I picked these up for you today," Mr. Thomas said, offering the packet, wrapped in brown butcher paper and tied with string.

"What . . . ?" The question was silly when an answer was so easy to find. Arnie carefully untied the string and unwrapped the package. And frowned in consternation. "I don't understand." Mr. Thomas's gift, if that was what it was, consisted of two pairs of gloves, one rather nice, if inexpensively made, pair sewn from what appeared to be soft kid, the other a much sturdier if less attractive pair made of some thick leather with the rough side exposed.

"Part of your education," Mr. Thomas said. Which Arnie considered to be an answer, but no explanation at all. "Put the black ones on. I had to guess at your size. If they're too far off, I can take them back tomorrow and exchange them."

Arnie shrugged. And did as he was told. The kid gloves, soft and of a fairly thin material, fit pretty well, tight now but with use he knew they would stretch to fit just fine.

"Excellent," Mr. Thomas said. "You have good hands. Much better than mine were. And you're going to be quick enough, I think. Mostly you need to learn the moves, and you are coming along well enough with that too."

Arnie looked at him, but didn't say anything. The past few afternoons, once Mr. Thomas got back to the boarding house from work, they'd gone over and over and over again the basic maneuvers of offensive and defensive strategy in the ring. Slowly, and bit by bit a little faster, and then faster again. Arnie was surprised at how easy the moves were coming to him after so little instruction.

"Now put the brown ones on."

"Yes, sir." Arnie tugged at the fingertips of the kid gloves to remove them.

"No, don't take those off, son. Put the others on over top of those."

"Sir?"

"That's right. The light pair, then the heavy ones on top of them."

Arnie shrugged and put the rough gloves on. "Perfect," Mr. Thomas said. The heavier brown gloves were larger than the kidskin ones and fit snug but comfortably over them.

"When the time comes," Mr. Thomas said, "when you think you will have to defend yourself, I want you to wear these gloves just like this, both of them together."

"I don't understand."

Mr. Thomas chuckled and said, "Of course not. So I'll tell you why. The black gloves—you can wear them alone if you have to and no one will think a thing about it—are to protect your hands. They'll keep you from getting cut up like I used to when I was fighting bare-knuckle style. You understand that, I'm sure."

"Yes, sir, but . . ."

Mr. Thomas's smile got wider. "The muleskin gloves," he said, "you see how they're made, the rough side exposed?"

Arnie nodded.

"I got a canvas water bag today too. Tomorrow I'll fill it with sand and start you working on that. What you want to do, see, is use these gloves to help stop your opponent."

Arnie tried to ask a question, but the fat man cut him off. "Give me a second here. I'll explain."

"Yes, sir."

"Remember how I told you to hit *through* your target?"

Arnie nodded, but Mr. Thomas reminded him of the instruction anyway. "You never punch for the nose of a man. You try to hit a point about four inches *behind* his nose. Then if the nose sort of gets in the way of your punch, well, it will land an awful lot harder."

"Yes, sir."

"Now I want you to add a little something to your motion. Just as you smack the guy—you don't do this when you're punching for the body, mind, just the head—just as your punch lands, I want you to twist your wrist. Like this. Roll your fist just a little bit. In either direction. That doesn't matter. Whatever feels comfortable to you. But you roll your fist just a little. Slow now, show me. Good, that's right. Twist it just the least bit as it lands. What that does, see, is it cuts the fellow. You want to do that especially when you're aiming for the eyebrows or the nose, or anywhere high on the head. You want to bloody him, you see. The more blood the better. For one thing, it's apt to flow into his eyes and blind him. A man can't fight you if he can't see you. And some men—more than you might think—can't abide the sight of their own blood. They see themselves all bloody and they figure they've already lost the fight." Mr. Thomas grinned. "And son, if a man once thinks he's lost a fight, then he has indeed been beaten."

"And these gloves . . . ?"

"Like I said, the thin ones help protect your hands, the muleskins help bloody the other man. And there's another purpose too. You'll notice both pair are in dark colors. That's what you want. The darker the better. That makes them more difficult to see, especially at night or any time the lighting is poor. Harder to see, and so, harder to anticipate, harder to block. That makes the fellow you're fighting think you're fast. Faster than him even if it doesn't happen to be so. But he'll believe you have fast hands, you see, and that's another thing to help him along toward thinking he's being beaten."

Arnie looked at the dark brown muleskin gloves, so innocent and ordinary in appearance, and realized he never would have thought of such a use for them on his own if he'd had half a year to chew on the subject. Protect one's own hands; bloody the other man to scare or temporarily blind him; make him believe you're quicker and more accurate than you really are. Yeah. It made sense.

"Tomorrow afternoon," Mr. Thomas said. "Tomorrow afternoon we'll start working on your punching. I already asked Mrs. Elroy. She said we can hang the bag in the buggy shed and take a couple lanterns out there so I can teach you in the evenings after supper. In the meantime, son, you can work on the footwork I showed you last night. You don't need me for that. Work on shuffling. Both feet moving. Never stepping, always dancing and shuffling, both forward or both back about the same time. You remember what I told you?"

"I remember."

"And light. Up on the balls of your feet. Never with your weight down on your heels. Up. Light. Like a moth circling around a flame. Move. Duck. Dig. You're getting it. You really are."

Arnie nodded. And looked at his new gloves again. Maybe he was beginning to get the feel of what Mr. Thomas was trying to teach him. Maybe he was after all. He grinned and made a fist, the movement inside the new leather unnatural and more difficult than it would be when the gloves were broken in. It occurred to him that there was one thing about the gloves that Mr. Thomas hadn't mentioned. There was something about the feel of them that made Arnie feel stronger and harder and just plain more able than usual. He made a fist again and smacked it hard into the palm of his other hand. The sound of it was loud on the soft evening air, and the gents at the far end of the porch, down where the light was better for the chess match, looked up from the game.

Arnie grinned at his mentor and friend. "Thanks," he said. "Thanks a lot."

Chapter Thirty-seven

"I think you're crazy," Andy told him.

"You've mentioned that before." He smiled. "More than once."

"Well, it's still true. That girl isn't worth—"

"She is to me," he said curtly, cutting her off before she could add anything more. Arnie already knew what Andy thought on the subject, and he didn't want to hear any more of it. Neither one of them was very likely to change their minds at this point, and Katherine Mulraney was a whole lot more important to Arnie than was Little Miss Snippet, Andrea Elroy.

He took a sip of the lemonade Andy had brought out to him on the porch when she came out to visit with him. Arnie looked rather hopefully up the street in the direction Mr. Thomas would come from on his way home from work. It was still a little early for him to arrive, but it was an excuse to divert the rather unpleasant direction the conversation was taking. And besides, he was eager for this evening's lesson. He was really beginning to get the hang of this fisticuffs business now, he thought. More importantly, Mr. Thomas thought so too. Or said he did. That was encouraging. Any day now he should be ready to go back and take on one of those toughs at the saloon. If he could only get one of them alone. Surely though he could find a way to do that. He would get one of them by himself and beat the truth out of the fellow, plain and simple.

"I wish you'd leave this whole thing alone," Andy insisted.

"We've already been over that. I'm going to find Katherine. I have to."

Andy opened her mouth to continue her argument—she was a stubborn little creature if nothing else—and again he cut her short. "Besides," he said, "there's something else I want to do."

"And what would that be?"

"Find out who told those guys to look for me. That first night I was in the city, remember? They knew who I was right away. I never told them anything nor asked them anything. I was just looking around, like, and they already knew who I was and where I came from and everything. Well, I want to find out how they could've known that."

"You never said anything to me about that before."

"Sure I did. You've forgotten."

"No, you didn't. I would have remembered. You must have talked about it with Mr. Thomas, but you never said anything to me. I would have figured it out if you had."

"You," he said, his voice heavy with sarcasm. After all, the dumb girl was, what? Twelve? Thirteen at the most? Sure, she'd have figured it out.

"Tell me what happened."

"I already did," he insisted.

"All right, then tell me again."

So he did. Going through it pretty much from the beginning. Getting into Denver on the train that day—had it only been a few weeks now? It seemed half of forever since he'd left home—and finding Chance Martingale, who really wasn't Martingale after all but a dumb salesman named Martin, and then going to look for Katherine and getting jumped by those guys and beaten up so awfully bad, and finally being lucky enough to end up with Mr. Thomas taking care of him. He went through it right from the get-go and he still hadn't any idea how those men would have been waiting for him.

"Arnie," the girl said with a shake of her head, "you really are a country hick, aren't you? You can't figure it out from what you just said?''

''No, and neither can you, smart aleck.''

''Of course I can. Anybody could if they put some thought to it.''

''Nonsense.''

''No, listen, I'm serious. This Mr. Martin has to have told them. He's the one who told you where to go next, where to look for . . . you know. That girl. He's the only person in the entire state of Colorado who could have known where you were going and what you looked like so those men would be watching for you.''

''But why would he do that?''

''I don't know. I mean, not for sure. Maybe he was afraid you would get the law after him for selling a girl into white slavery or something. That is against the law, I think. Even if it isn't, having everybody know about it, like if you caused a fuss, it wouldn't do his reputation any good. Something like that would ruin a man in this city. One who pretended to be respectable anyway. Or maybe he just didn't want to risk you telling his wife about the way he is when he's away from home selling whatever it is that he sells. It could be something as simple as that.''

''Look,'' Arnie said, ''I thought about all that too, but Martin couldn't have told them. There wasn't time for him to get to the saloon that evening and tell anyone about me. I mean, I went straight from his house to the saloon. He couldn't have gotten there ahead of me if he'd had a team and buggy all hitched up and waiting on him. I went straightway from the one place to the other. Got a ride on the streetcar and went right away. I was . . . in a hurry, you might say.''

''And that,'' the girl said emphatically, ''is why I'm telling you that you're a hayseed, Arnie. The man didn't have to go there himself. All he had to do was go to the nearest telephone and call ahead. Those other men would have known about you practically as soon as you were out of sight if he did that. It wouldn't have taken him two minutes. Not if there was a telephone available anywhere close by.''

''I never . . .''

"You never thought about the telephone, right?"

He nodded. She was right. Damned if she wasn't. He supposed he just wasn't, well, wasn't used to telephones and citified gimcracks, things like that. He supposed he really was a dumb hick and a hayseed like Andy said. So of course Claude Martin could have told them. Not only could have, *did*. Because Claude Martin was the only person anywhere who would have been *able* to tell them.

Which answered that question, thank goodness. Now to find out why Martin would have done such a thing . . . well, he'd just have to go back and ask the man a few more questions. Things like why he would have sicced those men on Arnie like a feist dog being sicced onto a thief.

And this time, dammit, Arnie did not intend to be so naive and gullible.

This time he would *make* Martin tell him the truth. Whatever it might be.

Chapter Thirty-eight

It had gotten so Arnie could remember the different trolleys that plied this particular route. The cars all looked about the same, of course, all of them painted alike and with the same lettering and stuff on the sides. And he paid no particular attention to the drivers and conductors. But the horses were different. There was one car pulled by a pair of almost-matched grays and one by a mismatched pairing of aging cobs and one where the nigh horse was blind in its off eye. And this car, with the short-coupled brown paired with a bobtailed bay horse. There were four cars on the route in all, and they made their circuit, from wherever to whatnot, in about an hour and twenty minutes, which meant there was one trolley or another coming along every twenty minutes or so.

Arnie knew that because he'd been loafing in the shade of a runty cottonwood since the middle of the afternoon, acting like a bummer waiting for someone to come along and offer him a job—and in fact he'd twice had to turn down offers of a good dinner in exchange for splitting stovewood or the like—and by now he was becoming more familiar with the Denver trolley system than he ever really wanted to be.

The trolley slowed and came to a fleeting halt, the driver not bothering to set his brakes despite the slight incline of the brick street here, and Claude Martin swung down off the step. The driver had a little mirror he could use to watch the side of the car with, and he was clucking his team forward even before Martin's foot hit the ground.

Claude Martin, dressed just as dapper and natty as ever in a fancy suit, and carrying a duckhead cane for good measure, came sauntering down the street like a man without a care in the world.

Arnie stepped out in front of him and all of a sudden Martin looked somewhat on the pale side. He'd been wrong. He did have some cares after all.

"You! What are you—?"

"You look surprised to see me, Claude. Or d'you prefer I should call you Chance?"

"I don't want you to call me anything. I just want you to get the hell away from me. Right now, or I'll call the police on you."

"You do that, Claude. Them and me will have a nice long talk about . . . things."

It scarcely seemed possible, but Martin became even whiter, his complexion pasty and not very healthy in appearance.

"First the police," Arnie said, "and then that nice wife of yours."

"You wouldn't."

"The hell I wouldn't," Arnie told him. "If you don't believe it, try me. And Claude, this time it won't do you any good to telephone to your friends down on Larimer Street. You hear what I'm telling you? This time I'm onto your tricks. An' this time I'm expecting some answers from you." Arnie smiled. And hoped the expression did not make him look friendly. If there was anything he did not want, it was to make friends with a miserable son of a bitch like this one in front of him.

"I never—"

"Of course you did."

"You can't prove—"

"Prove? Mister, I don't have to prove a damn thing to you. But do you know what? I bet I can bust your insides all to mush if I set in to thumping on you. Want to find out? Huh?" Arnie had never done such a thing before in his whole life, but he emphasized the threat with a jab of his forefinger into

the base of Claude Martin's throat. Just that was enough to
rock Martin back onto his heels and bring a rush of sweat onto
his forehead. What made Arnie uncomfortable, though, was
the idea that here he was being the one to start a fight. Or
trying to. He was the one bullying a smaller fellow, and as
long as he could remember he'd been told never to do any
such thing. A decent man—or boy, which was how his father
put it when he was little, back when the lessons were first
being drilled in—a decent man never struck a girl no matter
the provocation, never started a fight, never hit anybody
smaller, never . . . well, there was a long list of things a good
boy or a good man wasn't ever supposed to do. And here
Arnie was, not only picking on somebody smaller, but down
deep in his heart of hearts actually wanting the littler fellow
to take a swing at him. Or try and hit him with the cane or
. . . something, anything to give Arnie an excuse to haul off
and knock him halfway to tomorrow.

Martin used the sleeve of his handsome suitcoat to wipe
sweat off his lip, and visibly shuddered. "What . . . what do
you want of me?"

"Answers," Arnie told him. "Lots and lots of answers.
And this time, if you call ahead and try to get me busted up,
I'll know it's you I should call to account afterward. You hear
me, mister?"

"Yes, I . . . I do."

"Now let's you and me step over into the shade here so we
can have a nice talk." Arnie took Martin by the elbow and
gently led him off the street. Claude Martin followed along
just as meek as you please.

Chapter Thirty-nine

"By God, I can't believe you're back already," the bouncer named Karl told him. The other one, Colin, was seated there beside his pal, both of them enjoying an afternoon beer before the working stiffs commenced to get off shift and fill the place up for the evening. "You want to go a couple rounds, kid?"

Arnie opened his mouth to tell the big man that no, what he'd come for was information, not a fight. But suddenly he found himself grinning, and what came out wasn't that at all but, "As a matter of fact, mister, I'd like that real good. It'd give me a chance to get some back of what you gave me the other night."

"You're kidding me, right?"

"No, sir, I reckon not."

"Straight up?"

"Straight up, mister. Just the two of us." Arnie's grin got bigger. "Friendly like."

Karl laughed. "We don't do this for fun, sonny boy, just for money."

"And there I was thinking you was serious. Well, there's nothing I can do about it. I got no money to place as a wager to make it interesting to you."

Karl shrugged and took a long drink of his beer. His partner cocked his head to one side and squinted a mite while he gave Arnie a looking over. "Hell," Colin said, "I'll put up five bucks against your ten, Karl. What d'you say to that?"

"You'd bet against me?"

"At two to one, damn right."

"All right, you're on." Karl stood up. There were half a dozen, perhaps as many as eight early imbibers already in the saloon. In a loud voice, Karl announced to them, "Gents, we have a prizefight exhibition for you this afternoon. Me against this cowboy from Wyoming. The odds are two to one, and Lanny over at the bar there will hold the stakes. Anybody interested?"

They were, Arnie saw. Lordy, but they sure were. The few men who were sitting at tables in the place made a rush on the bar and even a couple fancy-dressed women—Arnie had no illusions now about what those ladies really were—came down from upstairs to join in the excitement.

Somehow word of the fight raced clean beyond the walls of the saloon, and men started coming in from the street despite the early hour. By the time quitting time rolled around, the place was filled with just about as many sweating bodies as the floor would hold, and there were more outside trying to get in. Apparently a fisticuffs contest was a popular event in Denver these days.

For sure Karl and his friends were taking the thing serious. They'd moved some of the gaming tables tight against the wall and used them to make two sides of a square ring, the other two consisting of chairs dragged away from the tables. Arnie judged the size of the ring to be twelve or fourteen feet to the side.

Why, they'd even provided stools and buckets and towels for each corner.

At some point it had been determined that Colin would stand in Arnie's corner to towel him off between rounds and give him water—or resuscitation—whenever he needed. A couple men Arnie didn't know were acting as Karl's seconds.

A man wearing a fine suit with a sparkling diamond stickpin in his tie and the emblem of a fraternal order in his lapel had come downstairs too and seemed to be more or less in charge of the goings-on. Arnie'd never seen him before either, but it was plain that this man was the boss of the whole shebang here.

"Are we ready, gents? Does everybody have a beer?" the boss asked of no one in particular. "If we're set then, Lanny, I want you to come take my watch and count the time between rounds." He tugged at his watch chain to produce a most handsome and obviously expensive stem-winding watch from his pocket along with a fob that was decorated with enough gold to hire two full hands for a month's work.

The boss handed his watch to the barman—by now two relief bartenders had showed up as if by magic and were busy as a pair of mice in a room full of cats trying to keep up with the demand for beer and the odd whiskey now and then. If nothing else, Arnie saw, his impulse was almighty good for business on an otherwise slow afternoon.

"You all know the rules," the boss announced. "A round lasts until a man leaves his feet. As soon as someone goes down, the time starts. The combatants," the word was new to him, but Arnie presumed that would mean Karl and him, "have one minute to toe the mark for the start of the next round."

"You got a mark?" someone in the crowd shouted out.

"The mark will be this yellow board right here," the boss answered, pointing it out with the toe of his highly polished shoe. "All right?"

"Just wanted to know," the same voice answered.

"That's fine. Are there any other questions?"

Arnie had one. "What about gloves? Can I keep my gloves on so I don't bust my skin open, sir? A man can't rope too good if his hands are messed up." Not that he expected to be doing any roping in the near future, but this man wouldn't know that. And Mr. Thomas had told him that bare knuckles used to be the rule but that gloves were becoming more and more common in prize rings nowadays.

"Do you have any objection to that, Karl?"

"I got no objections, Mr. Weaver. He can keep his gloves."

Weaver, Arnie thought. So he'd been right. This fellow was the owner of the saloon. And of certain other enterprises in the Larimer Street neighborhood. Good. Now Arnie knew who it was he had to talk to later.

"Do you want gloves, Karl?"

"Not me," Karl said, grinning and flexing his muscles for everybody to see.

Arnie wasn't real surprised. Another of the things Mr. Thomas told him was that most men believed—maybe it was true but maybe it wasn't—that a bare fist landed harder than a gloved one. It seemed only natural that Karl would want to fight that way then, especially since it was what he would already be accustomed to.

"That does it then, gentlemen. The contest will last until one of you fails to come to the mark. Is that agreed?"

Weaver gave Arnie a look and waited until he saw Arnie nod acceptance of the deal before he turned to Karl for his nod.

"Done," Weaver announced. "Seconds, we will waive the normal rule about stoppage of the fight by throwing your towel into the ring. I do not want anyone to think that the outcome might be influenced by the fact that participants in both corners are my employees. Is that understood and agreed to?"

Arnie nodded, and so did Colin. On the other side of the ring, Karl and his people did too.

"Very well. Fighters, prepare yourselves."

Colin helped Arnie out of his shirt—it wasn't easy trying to manage the buttons with two pair of gloves on his hands—and gave his chest a swipe with the towel, even though he wasn't sweaty yet. Karl was already stripped to the waist and looking plenty fit and ready.

"Very well, gentlemen." Weaver motioned to Lanny and the barman/timekeeper used a metal ladle to clang the bottom of a pot he'd gotten from someplace. The buzz of conversation that had filled the saloon died away to near silence, and Weaver said, "If both corners are ready . . . gentlemen, toe the mark, please."

Arnie swallowed. Hard. There was a butterfly flutter down inside his belly somewhere as he stepped forward. This thing had gotten way out of hand from what he'd first proposed, and he hoped to hell he knew what he was doing.

135

Chapter Forty

Karl was strong and confident, older and much more experienced than Arnie would ever be, and seemed very much at ease here inside a prize ring.

Arnold Rasmussen was . . . scared half to death. Off to the side, Lanny beat on the bottom of the tin pot and Karl smacked Arnie with a stinging left hand that sprang out of nowhere and snapped Arnie's head back.

All the things Mr. Thomas taught him, all the practicing they'd done, all the hours of shuffling his feet and whacking the punching bag and learning to block and duck and move and dance . . . all that went clean out of his head with the sound of that ladle beating on the soup pot.

Arnie lifted his hands, not in the approved and effective style he'd been shown, but simply trying to put wrists and forearms and elbows between his already aching jaw and Karl's punches.

Arnie might as well not have bothered trying to defend himself. It was obvious even to Arnie that Karl was in no hurry for this fight to end. The older and more experienced man took his time. Moving. Setting up. Selecting the places he wanted to hit and then whistling blows past, around, and through Arnie's inept defense to land with sharp, painful power on Arnie's jaw or temple or nose.

Arnie's nose went early in the round. He could hear a sort of muted crunch, and a bright scarlet gout of blood sprayed

Karl's chest and belly. The blood ran down Karl's hairy stomach and onto the man's trousers, soiling them from the waist down to the crotch.

Ha! Arnie thought sourly to himself. Served the son of a bitch right to have his pants ruined. Helluva way to accomplish that, though.

Karl saw the blood—well, everyone in the place was sure to; it would have been rather difficult to miss it—and bore in to follow that measure of success with more of the same. He continued to pummel Arnie's face and bleeding nose with one blow after another.

By then, mercifully enough, Arnie's entire face was numb from the punishment already inflicted. He heard the punches land and he felt them in a dull and distant sort of way. But really, and oddly, there was no actual pain involved. That would come soon enough, of course, once the shock wore off, but for the moment he was immune from the sting of Karl's blows.

Behind the two men, over them, all around them, Arnie was aware of a sort of presence. Almost a tangible pressure. It was the collective voice of the crowd, the nobs and players shouting insults or encouragement depending on the way their money had been laid. The voices blended together into a loud, liquid whole that surrounded the fighters and overflowed the senses. It was like nothing Arnie had ever experienced before. And nothing he wanted to know ever again.

Arnie himself had a fleeting thought that he probably should have placed a wager himself. On Karl. If he'd had any money, that is.

Karl hit him again and Arnie's head jerked sharply enough to make his neck hurt. Dammit, he wished Karl would quit doing that.

"Down," he heard a voice somewhere behind him, coming somehow out of the general cacophony of the crowd to find him. "Go down, you idiot." Arnie was reasonably sure the advice was intended for him. There was nothing to suggest that Karl might be the first to go down. Not unless the man slipped on Arnie's blood and lost his footing, that is. "Go down, Rasmussen, down!"

137

It likely was good advice. It would end the round and give him a minute in which to gather both his wits and his breath. He understood the wisdom of that idea. Still, Arnie couldn't do it. He hadn't stepped into this ring with the idea of losing. Never mind that he was doing a pretty good job of that. He resented and resisted it, and if Karl was to beat him again, damn him, he would have to earn it.

Which, in truth, he was doing right well.

Karl backed away, grinned, and dropped his guard to survey the damage done thus far. Arnie should have gone after him then. He knew he should. But he didn't. Instead he stood, head down and spirits sagging, gulping for the breath that he could not seem to get.

"All right, kid. Let's get this over with, what d'you say?"

Karl hunched his shoulders and lifted his fists once more as he moved closer now, with every apparent intention of this time doing serious hurt.

Arnie stood mute and immobile, waiting like a tired old ewe ready for slaughter.

Chapter Forty-one

Arnie threw a punch of his own as Karl came near—he could not honestly remember if that was his first of the fight, although surely he would have at least tried to hit Karl before now—then hurriedly ducked in a desperate attempt to ward off the counterpunch that came in behind Arnie's wildly missing right hand.

His foot hit a slick spot on the floor, his own blood perhaps, or the contents of an overturned cuspidor or schooner of beer, and before Karl's punch could land, Arnie found himself on his butt. Hitting the floor like that stung his tailbone and jarred his aching head.

"Time," he heard Mr. Weaver shout, and Karl stopped short of finishing the fight with the big right he had cocked and ready to deliver. "Time."

Someone, probably Colin, grabbed Arnie from behind, lifting him bodily to his feet and guiding him into a corner of the makeshift ring, where a stool and bucket were waiting.

"Here, kid." Colin shoved a beer mug into Arnie's heavily gloved hands and began wiping Arnie's face and chest with a dampened towel. The beer cleansed his throat and the wet towel felt cool and refreshing on his skin, but apart from those two small bright spots, Arnie felt pretty much like Hell warmed over.

"I thought you'd do better than that, kid," Colin told him. "I really did."

"Sorry."

"Don't apologize, damn it. *Do* something. I taught you better than this. You're embarrassing me."

Arnie turned to look in the direction of this new voice. It was Mr. Thomas. He'd come into the saloon and somehow made his way through the loudly buzzing mob to join Colin in Arnie's corner.

"Use your hands like I taught you, son. Remember your footwork and—"

Lanny beat on the pot again, calling the fighters to the mark.

"Ten seconds, kid," Colin reminded him. "You have ten seconds to get out there. Unless you want to quit."

Arnie scowled. And shook his head. Grimly he forced his aching body upright and, hunching his shoulders and swinging his arms to loosen his muscles, marched into the center of the ring, where Karl was already waiting with the tip of his left shoe poised on the yellowish floorboard they'd agreed would be the mark.

"I'm surprised, kid. You got more guts than I expected," Karl said in a low voice that barely carried over the noise of the crowd. Then the man laughed and added, "Either that or you're dumber than I thought you were. You coulda stayed in your corner and avoided taking any more, you know."

"Mister, I haven't even started yet," Arnie said, amazing even himself. Of course, the statement was true enough, if only because Arnie had yet to accomplish a single lousy thing.

"Your choice, kid, but don't blame me if you get hurt."

Arnie nodded and positioned his toe at the edge of the yellow board.

"Don't think," he heard Mr. Thomas shout behind him. "Let your training take over. Lift your hands and let your muscles do what we taught them."

Arnie grunted a silent acknowledgment that was intended for his own resolve and lifted his hands into the silly-looking but highly effective posture Mr. Thomas had shown him.

Chapter Forty-two

Arnie looked into Karl's eyes. And remembered. Watch the eyes, Mr. Thomas had taught him. There were some who said you should watch the other man's shoulders. Some said the head. Mr. Thomas said he always watched the other fellow's eyes.

But never, Mr. Thomas said they all agreed, never watch the other man's hands. By the time you saw them move, it was already too late to do anything about it.

All through that first miserable round, Arnie realized, he'd been mesmerized by the sight of Karl's hands. And he'd gotten his clock cleaned right thoroughly.

Now Arnie looked into the older man's eyes. And knew.

The instant Lanny banged on the pot, Karl threw a punch, a darting straight right that was headed for Arnie's battered nose.

Huh! Not that easy, damn you, Arnie thought. Karl punched and Arnie let Mr. Thomas's training take over. Without particularly thinking about it, he flicked his left wrist to intercept Karl's fist and deflect it harmlessly to the side.

Arnie shuffled forward half a step and jabbed with his left, occupying the space vacated by Karl's errant punch. Arnie's fist landed square on Karl's nose, his aim not for the nose itself but for a point about four inches behind it, so that the flat of his fist punched through and not onto Karl's flesh.

He heard a peculiarly satisfying crunch of gristle giving

way, and this time the spray of blood was not his own.

Karl backed off, his eyes glistening with sudden moisture as tears filled them in the body's automatic response to the punishment.

Arnie shuffled forward, light on the balls of his feet, never losing his balance, never coming down flat-footed, where he could be caught as if rooted to the floor.

Karl feinted with a left, then threw a hard left hook. Arnie swayed to the side so as to make the punch sail harmlessly by, then stepped forward and banged a solid right onto the shelf of Karl's jaw, throwing the man's head to the side and staggering him.

Arnie hadn't remembered to give his fist that little twist at the end like Mr. Thomas had taught him. He berated himself for the lapse and next time remembered as he delivered another right onto Karl's forehead, just over his left eyebrow.

The technique worked just like Mr. Thomas said it should. Skin parted under the rough mulehide of Arnie's glove, and blood began to seep into the caterpillar fur of the bouncer's eyebrow.

Arnie did it again. And a third time. The blood flowed more freely as each succeeding punch further opened the cut, and it was quickly apparent that Karl was beginning to have difficulty seeing.

Karl threw a wild left, guessing at where Arnie could be behind the curtain of red that interfered with his vision, and Arnie tattooed him with a stinging combination of sharp lefts followed by a crunching right hand. Karl staggered, slipped, went down hard.

"Time," Mr. Weaver called.

Arnie stopped himself from punching, turned, and went back to his corner, where Colin and Mr. Thomas waited. There was a considerable difference between the way he felt this time and the way he'd felt at the end of the first round.

The crowd obviously sensed it too. Their roar was all the louder and more boisterous, and Arnie could hear someone collecting a fresh round of spirited betting.

"That's better," Mr. Thomas said. "No, don't swallow that, dammit. Rinse your mouth and spit it out. You don't need your brains addled any more than that fellow's already made them.''

Arnie swished the beer inside his mouth and spit it into the bucket Mr. Thomas held for him, while Colin swabbed his face and chest with the equally refreshing wet towel.

"You're doing all right, kid. Better than I'd hoped. You want some advice?"

"Sure."

"Go for his gut now. Karl's soft in the belly. That will take the starch right outa him."

"I thought Karl was your friend," Arnie said.

"Hell, he is, kid, but if I'm gonna be in your corner, I'm gonna be on your side, right?" He grinned. "Besides, I got money on you, boy. Of course I want you to come through for me."

Lanny clanged the bottom of the pot, and Mr. Weaver shouted, "Time, gentlemen, time! Come to the mark now if you please."

Arnie grabbed at the beer mug and took a brief sip to cut the phlegm in his throat, then jumped up off his stool and went light on his feet into the center of the ring, where Mr. Weaver was waiting.

He felt good now. Strong.

Across the way, Karl did not look nearly so tough and invulnerable as he had just a little while earlier.

In fact, Arnie thought that Karl looked a mite pale and nervous at the start of this third round.

Chapter Forty-three

"That man is going to live forever," Arnie said with considerable feeling.

"What?" Colin rubbed the towel over Arnie's face and chest. "Why'd you say that?"

"Because he's too damn tough to ever die. Why won't he stay down, dammit?"

"Would you, kid?"

Arnie shook his head. Hell no, he wouldn't. And neither would Karl. Pride kept driving the man back into the center of the ring time after time, even though the rounds were becoming almighty short now, and his face looked more like raw meat than human skin.

The blood from ugly gashes over both eyes could hardly be stanched between rounds any longer, and it was a wonder Karl could stay on his feet. He wobbled forward on rubber knees, though, every time Lanny banged the tin pot.

"You're doing fine, son," Mr. Thomas told him. "Keep working the body."

"Yes, sir."

The gong sounded, and Arnie moved out into the ring. He had to work at making it look light and easy. His own legs were weary now, and he could guess at how Karl's must feel.

Even so, the professional bouncer—Arnie had developed too much respect for the older man's courage at this point to think of Karl as being a bullyboy—came off his stool and staggered forward in response to Lanny's clanging call to the mark.

"Ready, gents? All right now." Weaver nodded, and Lanny banged the pot again.

Karl stood there. Swaying. His eyes unfocused and his hands at his sides. He looked tired.

Well, Arnie thought, he was damned well entitled. Arnie was exhausted himself. And he wasn't the one who'd been taking punishment these last . . . how many rounds had there been? Arnie could not remember. Fifteen? Sixteen? Somewhere in that neighborhood, he thought. He would have to remember to ask Mr. Thomas after this round. If it ever got started.

Karl was still standing in front of him, making no effort to defend himself, his big, blood-smeared body moving from side to side as he fought to keep his balance.

There was nothing to prevent Arnie from dropping him now. No defense at all. Karl stood there with a bovine look on him. Quiescent and vulnerable.

Arnie poised himself for a knockout blow. Raised his right hand and cocked it, set to fly.

He held back. Waited. This wasn't sporting, damn it. It was as much a contest of fisticuffs now as being the poleax man in a slaughterhouse was hunting. In neither case was the quarry in any position to resist.

Arnie looked at Mr. Weaver and raised his eyebrows. "Sir, do I have to do this?"

Karl answered the question before his boss had to. The gutsy bouncer's legs finally gave out, and he toppled face forward onto the saloon floor.

Weaver did not bother with the formality of counting the minute down. The saloon owner grabbed Arnie's left hand and held it high over his head. "The winner!" he shouted, and a huge roar of approval mingled with no small amount of anguish rushed through the crowd as bettors began anticipating spending their winnings. Or bemoaning their losses.

There would be, Arnie suspected, a hell of a lot more losers than winners present.

Not that it mattered. Not really. Arnie knelt and began trying to help Karl revive.

Chapter Forty-four

Mr. Weaver, who owned the saloon and the girls and heaven knew what else, nodded in the direction of the stairway and said, "Bring the kid and his manager, Colin."

"Yes, sir. Uh, sir? What about Karl?"

"When he feels up to it."

"You aren't gonna—?"

"Of course not, Colin. Karl still has his job. Come along now with these gentlemen, will you? Lanny, take care of Karl." Weaver mounted the stairs without bothering to look back. But then Arnie felt sure the boss knew he had no need to worry about whether his instructions were being followed. He could likely count on having whatever he wanted, at least under this roof.

"Kid?" Colin pointed after his employer. "You too Mister . . . um. . . ."

Mr. Thomas introduced himself, then poked Arnie in the back and motioned him upstairs.

Arnie recovered his shirt first and pulled it on. He removed his gloves and stuffed them into a back pocket so he could manage the shirt buttons, then retrieved his wide-brimmed hat and finally followed Mr. Weaver to the second floor of the establishment. It was the first time Arnie had ever climbed those stairs. There was a smell in the air up there that cut through the saloon odors from down below. This was stronger. Perfume. And powder.

147

The girls who worked up here remained out of sight for the most part, but now that he was close enough to be assaulted with those strong scents, he knew Claude Martin hadn't lied this time. At least when it came to telling him what it was that went on up here. Arnie looked at a closed and unrevealing door leading into one of the very private rooms—judging from how close together the doors were set, he realized that the rooms must be tiny in their proportions, the better to put as many of them as possible into the available space—and blushed just from thinking about the things that might well be going on inside, even at that very moment.

"Down to the end, then right," Colin said.

The relatively open balcony, from which one could look down onto the saloon floor, led into a short hallway. Inside that there was another door no different from the others save that this one stood open.

"Go on inside."

Arnie did. And found himself in a part of the place he hadn't suspected existed. Obviously Mr. Weaver owned the entire building, not just the saloon portion of it, for his office and whatever else was back here extended beyond the walls of the saloon below to occupy the space over the top of whatever business was beside the saloon as well. Arnie tried to recall what that business was but could not. Not for sure.

"Welcome," Weaver said. The businessman was seated already, an expanse of polished rosewood between himself and his guests now as the gentleman greeted them from behind his desk.

There were handsome paintings on the walls—tasteful scenes of mountains and meadows, Arnie saw, and not the girly drawings his imagination might have suggested—and a fine rug on the floor. The furniture was hand-carved and obviously expensive.

"Have a seat. Please."

Arnie took the chair indicated, and Mr. Thomas sat beside him. Colin, Arnie noticed, remained standing, placing himself behind the other guests so he was in a position to defend his boss in the unlikely event such a need should arise.

"Allow me to introduce myself. T. Emerson Weaver, at your service. And you are . . . ?"

Arnie and Mr. Thomas gave their names and received warm smiles in return. "A pleasure to make your acquaintances, both of you," Weaver said. "Mr. Thomas."

"Yes?"

"Are you Mr. Rasmussen's manager, sir?"

"Just a friend."

"I see. Then you have no intention to put the young man on the road in competitive events of some sort?"

Mr. Thomas rubbed his chin. "No, I hadn't thought to do that. But now that you mention it, the idea doesn't sound too bad, does it."

"If the two of you do make that determination," Weaver said, "I might be willing to bankroll the venture, provide travel and living expenses and the like. Even set you up with certain contacts that might be, ahem, advantageous." He smiled. "For a percentage of the take, of course."

"The lad and I will discuss it later, but the decision will naturally be his."

"No need to talk about it now or later, not when there's something I have to do before I can think of anything else," Arnie put in, not so sure he wanted Mr. Thomas taking a hand in deciding his future. And damn sure not wanting Mr. Weaver making up his mind for him.

"Ah, yes," Weaver said, still smiling. "That would be the girl, of course."

Arnie blinked. "You know about that?"

"Certainly. Poor Martingale has telephoned me several times about you. This afternoon he sounded positively frantic with worry."

"He has reason to be scared," Arnie said grimly. Dammit, he'd told Martin *not* to call here again but the man went and did it anyway.

"So I see from your performance downstairs. Incidentally, young fellow, I hope you will accept my apologies for the rude way you were received on your first, um, visit."

"Oh, you mean . . ." Yes. Of course he did. Colin and Karl and a whole lot of pain.

"Martingale said you meant to cause trouble. He warned me against you."

"I don't want no trouble, Mr. Weaver. Didn't then and don't now. I just want to get Katherine safe back home where she belongs."

"I see. Katherine. Is that her real name then?"

"Yes, sir. Katherine Mulraney. Of Alder Creek, Wyoming. That's where I'm from too."

"Uh-huh. Katherine. She went by a slightly different name here. As is common. I doubt any of these girls wants to remember the names they were born with, poor things. I do what I can to keep them safe and in a comfortable environment, you know. All my ladies are treated with courtesy and respect. As your Katherine was also."

Arnie felt his heart sink. It had only this past minute or so come up into his throat when Mr. Weaver acknowledged knowing Katherine. But now there was something . . . he realized then what it was. Weaver said Katherine "was" treated respectfully, not that she "is" getting good care in the saloon. Like as if she wasn't around any more. All Arnie's suddenly renewed hopes were dashed. If she wasn't here any longer . . .

Chapter Forty-five

"I feel I owe you something, Mr. Rasmussen. After all, you turned a dull and very slow afternoon into an exciting and profitable one. May I ask if, well, if you came out healthy with your wagering just now?"

"You mean on the fight, sir? Oh, I didn't have any money bet on myself."

"Surely you didn't bet on Karl and then win anyway?" Weaver asked.

Arnie laughed. "I might be from the sticks, sir, but I'm not that dumb. I didn't bet 'cause I didn't have the wherewithal to lay a wager."

"Arnie," Mr. Thomas put in, "there are a few things I didn't teach you. I felt there was no need under the circumstances, since we hadn't thought about you fighting professionally. But Mr. Weaver did not mean to imply you were dumb. He is really asking if you're a tanker."

"A what?"

"A pro who pretends to be a country bumpkin but isn't. You see, one of the ways certain people might choose to increase a payout would be for the fighter to place a bet against himself. If the whispers got around about that, you see, everyone would think the fighter's intention was to throw the fight, to lose intentionally. Then naturally everyone would put their money on the other man. And the tanker then comes on strong and collects long odds on bets placed by someone else, called

a ringer. Mr. Weaver was asking if you put one over on him.''
Thomas looked at Weaver and raised an eyebrow. ''I assume
you had some money on your man?''

''Naturally. I've seen Karl fight. But I didn't lose so much
that I mind giving it up to an honest effort.''

''The boy doesn't know the ropes, Mr. Weaver. He's just
exactly what he seems.''

Weaver thought about that for a moment, then shrugged.
''You know, Mr. Thomas, I believe that he is.'' The gentleman
opened a desk drawer and brought out a coin purse, from
which he extracted a gleaming twenty-dollar double eagle. He
leaned forward to lay it on the edge of his desk in front of
Arnie. ''I admire your pluck, son, and I don't want you walking away from here broke. You said you hadn't money to bet
with. I feel obligated to take care of that problem.''

''But you lost money on the fight your own self,'' Arnie
protested. ''That isn't fair, sir.''

Weaver laughed. ''Son, I'm sure I made much more in sales
and in future good will than I lost from betting on my man
Karl. Why, half the men downstairs were in here for the first
time this afternoon. They had a good time and were treated
fairly. Most of them will come back. You've not only in-
creased my profits today, Mr. Rasmussen, you've added to my
customer base. Let me reward you for that. Believe me, I will
suffer no loss because of it.''

''If it's all the same to you, sir, what I really want is to
know where I can find Katherine. I take it she's no longer,
uh . . .'' He didn't know quite how to finish that sentence without becoming indelicate.

''Staying here?'' Weaver asked.

''Yes, sir. Thank you.''

''Unfortunately she is not, or I would have had her brought
in to see you before now, believe me.''

''Do you know where I might find her, sir?''

''Colin?''

''Don't ask me, boss. I never talk with any of those—''

''Ask around, will you? She may have said something to
one of the other, um, young ladies.'' Weaver looked back at

Arnie and smiled. "Your Miss Mulraney chose to end her stay here. That was a decision made of her own free will. I never try to hold any of my girls beyond their will, you understand."

"Yes, sir."

"If she formed any friendships, with any of the other girls say, or with any of my employees, Colin will find out about it. Anything he learns about where she may have gone from here he will pass along to you. Is that fair?"

"Yes, sir, it is, thank you."

"And Mr. Thomas."

"Yes?"

"Think about what I said earlier. If you and young Mr. Rasmussen want to make the tour, my offer still stands. I would gladly bankroll you and make the introductions. We could all turn a tidy profit, I think. The boy has potential." The gent shook his head. "He looks so damned young and innocent, doesn't he? But he punches like a mule kicks. Think about it, Mr. Thomas. Talk to him. Why, with a little experience he might someday be as good as you were in your prime."

"You remember that?" Thomas asked, his voice betraying no small amount of pleasure that his own long-past days in the ring should be brought back to mind by this gentleman.

"Baby-faced Brad Thomas? Of course I remember. I won more than a few dollars backing you against bigger, harder-looking men. But that was when we were both younger, wasn't it? Now there is a new generation taking over where you and I left off."

"Yes, that is the truth, isn't it."

"Colin, see that you find out everything the other girls know about Irish Katie. Mr. Rasmussen, anything there is to learn, Colin should know by this time tomorrow. You can talk to him directly at that time. Now if you would all excuse me, I have work to do." The boss smiled. And turned his attention to a sheaf of papers taken from a box on his desk.

Arnie and Mr. Thomas made their way out, Arnie trembling

slightly from the hope that now, with the help of Mr. Weaver, he might soon again find Katherine and tell her about the hope, the future, the renewed respectability that he had to offer.

Tomorrow. Colin would tell him tomorrow.

Chapter Forty-six

The bar was still full. Not quite as packed as before the fight perhaps, but still much busier than usual at this after-work hour.

"How came you to be here, Mr. Thomas? I didn't expect you to see my first fight. Heck, I didn't expect to see it my own self. It just kind of happened," Arnie said as they hurried outside. There was still time for them to get home to the boarding house for supper.

"I stop in most evenings after work. If you'll recall, this is where I first met you. And when I saw what was going on, well, I had to help in your corner, didn't I."

"I'm awful glad you were there. Thanks."

They walked down to Colfax Avenue, to the closest trolley stop. The next trolley was already in sight.

"Before I forget," Mr. Thomas said, "here." He dipped two fingers into his vest pocket and brought out a gold coin.

"What's that?"

"The money Weaver gave you. You forgot it when you left his office."

"I didn't forget it, Mr. Thomas. I left it there apurpose. I didn't earn it."

"You earned it, son. You earned it." He tucked it into Arnie's pocket, and Arnie did not protest any further. After all, Mr. Thomas hadn't earned the money either, and if one of them was going to have it, it might as well be Arnie.

155

"What will you do now, son?" Mr. Thomas asked.

"You know the answer to that already."

"I can't talk you out of it?"

"No, sir, I expect not."

"You would marry the woman?"

"Woman? She's not but seventeen."

Mr. Thomas gave him a long, sad look. "Arnie, that girl, as you call her, is older now than you will ever be. Take my word on that."

"No matter," Arnie said. "She was done wrong. I intend to make it right for her. That includes marrying her if she'll have me, for that would surely put her back on good terms with her folks. And there's nobody for a hundred miles around would say anything bad against the Rasmussens, not one of us. We have a good name, earned with hard work and honest dealings. Everybody that knows us knows that about us. My pap wouldn't have it any other way."

"That, son, I can believe."

The trolley came to a halt in front of them, and Mr. Thomas prodded Arnie off the curb and into the car.

Tomorrow, Arnie kept thinking. Tomorrow evening Colin should be able to tell him where Katherine was.

If, that is, she'd confided in any friends at the saloon.

Please God, Arnie pleaded under his breath, please let her have told somebody what she intended to do after she left Mr. Weaver's place.

Chapter Forty-seven

Arnie was back at Weaver's saloon by noon. They'd said Colin would have the information—or not—by late afternoon. Arnie couldn't wait that long. He got to the place while the lunch crowd was still there.

And he was yet standing there at the bar, waiting and fidgeting, when the evening after-work crowd started coming in. There had been no sign of Colin all afternoon, and Lanny the bartender professed not to have seen him that day.

Even so, there was no chance, none whatsoever, that Arnie would become discouraged and leave. If he had to stand right there the whole night long, he intended to be there when Colin finally showed up.

Which happened about seven or so that evening. Colin and Karl came down the stairs together, Karl looking somewhat the worse for wear.

"There you are, kid. I told Karl you'd be here. He wanted to see you."

Arnie shifted from one foot to the other a trifle nervously. If Karl wanted to take offense at the fact that he'd lost a fair fight . . .

That wasn't it at all. Karl held a big hand out for Arnie to shake, a rather sheepish grin on his face. "You do all right, kid," the bouncer said. "I don't think anybody's ever hit me so hard as you did."

"Are you all right now?"

"Oh, hell yes. You didn't do nothing that won't heal. Except maybe to my pride. I thought sure I could take you."

"What really hurt him," Colin put in, "was having to pay off the bet he placed with me. Ten bucks at two to one. And at that he was lucky. Odds after the first round got as high as six to one against you."

"Look, fellas, this is all real interesting, but . . ."

"But it ain't what you came to hear, right?"

Arnie nodded.

"Karl, whyn't you bring us three beers, and—"

"Why should I be the one to spring for the beer?" Karl demanded.

"Because you're the one came up short last night. Now hush and let me have a word with Rasmussen, will you?"

Karl grumbled loudly—but turned his head and winked at Arnie where Colin couldn't see—then headed for the bar.

"Over here," Colin suggested. "This table looks kinda private."

"Do you know—?"

"The truth is, kid, I'm not sure. Your girl didn't have any real friends amongst those pigs upstairs. I mean, you don't know them, but they ain't much. You know how you hear stories about whores with hearts of gold? About Silver Heels and girls like that that everybody loves because they nurse fellas back to life in epizootics and all like that?"

Arnie nodded. Everybody heard tales like that, even in Alder Creek. Even the name Silver Heels was familiar to him. She'd been a soiled dove in some camp down here in Colorado and was said to have saved dozens of lives during an outbreak of the influenza, maybe hundreds.

"Listen to what I'm telling you, kid. Don't believe any of that crap. I know whores. I mean, I ought to. I work around enough of them, right?"

"I . . . sure, if you say so."

"I do say so, and I'm telling you that there's no such thing as a whore with a heart of gold. They're all stupid and lazy and most of them are mean as snakes to boot. Don't never trust one of them. They'll lie to you even when it'd be to their advantage to tell the truth. Don't you ever trust one of them."

"No, sir." In truth Arnie had never known one of that sort. Didn't much expect to either.

"Anyway, I asked around. The answers I got should be fairly straight, because I made it plain it was Mr. Weaver that wanted this thing cleared up. Otherwise I know they wouldn't any of them have told me a word I could've believed enough to pass on to you.

"The bad part of it is that your girl Irish Katie—"

"Katherine," Arnie corrected.

"Right. Katherine, she didn't have any real friends amongst those sows upstairs. Which shows pretty good judgment, I suppose. But which also means there wasn't anybody that she confided in before she ran away."

"Ran away?" Arnie asked. "The girls are free to come or go as they please, right? That's what Mr. Weaver said yesterday."

"A figure of speech," Colin said. "So to speak."

Arnie shrugged. Karl joined them with three brimming mugs in his hands. Arnie noticed that Karl had been poured beer with practically no head on it, while any time he'd bought beer here, the foamy head was always generous enough to take up a good quarter of the mug. Colin and Karl took time to dip their beaks, but Arnie's sat untouched on the table. It wasn't beer he'd come here for this evening.

"Anyway, like I was saying, your Katherine didn't exactly tell anybody where she was going. But for a couple days before she took off, she'd been asking questions about a new strike—silver, I think—somebody made up near Fairplay, Alma, somewhere around there."

Neither name was familiar to Arnie. But they didn't have to be. Wherever they were, if Katherine was there he would find them. "New strike, you say."

"That's right. I forget the name of the place now. Karl?"

"Mosquito Gulch, that's what they call it. South of Mosquito Pass, I think it is. That's the pass that lies between Alma on this side of the mountain and Leadville over on the other. I know about that 'cause I used to work in a mine outside Fairplay. There's been a road through there for a long time, but I never heard of anybody finding ore bodies up that way until this past couple months. Now they say there's a fair-sized town growing. Of course it could go bust next week, but right now it's supposed to be hot.''

"And this Mosquito Gulch. You think that's where Katherine went?''

"It's where she was asking about, I know that. But I can't promise you for certain sure that she went there. She could've gone anyplace once she slipped outa here, you know. She had some money on her. She stole forty dollars from Brown Bessie before she took off, and that Charleen girl—you know the one, Karl—she claims to have lost a brooch that her mama.gave to her.'' Colin laughed. "Which prob'ly means she stole it herself off some other girl and is mad because Irish—I mean Katherine—has it now.''

Arnie tried to ignore the accusations that Katherine might have stolen anything. She wouldn't do a thing like that. He knew she wouldn't.

Besides, he reminded himself, the whores upstairs all lied. Colin said that his own self not five minutes earlier. You couldn't trust them when they claimed something ugly like that.

"I expect the only thing I can do,'' Arnie said, "is go and take a look. If she's there, I'll find her.''

"Kid, can I give you a word of advice? I know you haven't asked for it, but me and Karl here, we like you. You're all right. You stand up in front of a man and you don't go running to the coppers, and we don't either one of us want to see you come to no harm.''

"That's generous of you. But if you're going to tell me to go home instead of—''

"No, I expect we know better'n that by now. You'll go. Likely you'll even find her. But . . . Arnie, don't put your hopes too high. You know what I'm telling you?''

"I'm not sure that I do, Colin.''

"I think the reason she ran off from here is that she didn't want you to find her, kid. She knew you were looking for her. We all did after that son of a bitch Martingale got scared of you. You do know that that's why we was laying for you that first time you come in, don't you?''

Arnie nodded.

"Right. Well, Irish knew it too. The word went around fast. She could've come downstairs and talked to you any time she had a mind to, but she didn't want to face you. Whatever is between you two—and me, I don't even want to know what that could be—she didn't want to see you again. She wanted shut of you and she wanted shut of Wyoming, and I think she'd have been content enough upstairs if it hadn't been for not wanting you to find her. I mean . . . how the hell can I put this . . . she's one of them that fits right into the sportin' life."

"Sporting life?"

"That's what they call it, the pimps and the hustlers and the whores. Not that there's any sport in it, but they call it that."

Arnie frowned. "I know what a whore is, of course, and a pimp. What's a hustler?"

"A hustler is a come-on girl. She cadges drinks off the gents—you don't wanta hear the names they got for the paying customers; some of them are pretty crude and insulting, never mind that you'd think they'd appreciate the poor saps that keep them in the dough—and the guy buying the drinks gets charged for a fancy beverage, but all the girl is really drinking is colored water or cold tea or like that. But the guy pays for high-priced wines, even champagne and stuff like that. It's a hustle is what it is."

"And these girls, do they . . . I mean, they aren't like the whores, right? All they have to do is get the guy to buy expensive drinks?"

"Some go for more than that, some don't. It depends."

Arnie latched onto that idea like a brook trout rising to a fly. Of course. Katherine hustled drinks for a living. Not . . . the other stuff. Hustling was bawdy and daring and all, but it was within the bounds of what she would allow herself to do. The other stuff wasn't. Arnie knew that. And this was all right. He felt considerably better now.

"Anyway, kid," Colin rambled on, "you mind what I've told you. These girls are no damn good. And Irish—Katherine—she don't want you to find her. You might think about allowing her some privacy. At least give her the chance to walk away on her own terms. You know? Check her from a distance to see that she's all right, then go home. You can tell her folks something that will ease their minds, and that will be that.'' Colin smiled. ''Think about it.''

Arnie nodded, grateful for the man's interest and concern, but with no notion whatsoever of taking that advice. Nor did he blurt out that his intention was not merely to check up on Katherine, but to marry her. For that, he was sure, was the only way he could rescue her from her sense of shame after what Claude Martin did to her, damn him.

''Thanks,'' he told Colin and his pal Karl. ''This sounds strange even to me, but I'm glad I met you and that things worked out between us. You fellows are all right.''

''So are you, Rasmussen. Good luck to you.''

Arnie shook their hands and left the saloon. He had some packing to do.

Chapter Forty-eight

Saying good-bye was almost as hard as it'd been when he left his own blood family behind. Arnie hadn't expected that, but it was so. Why, it was even difficult saying good-bye to Andrea and her dang dog.

"You'll come back, won't you?" Andy asked, the little dog lying in the crook of her elbow and a smudge of flour—she must have been helping her mother bake biscuits for the evening meal—on her nose.

"Sure I will," Arnie promised, not sure if he meant that or not. Probably so, really. He owed Mr. Thomas for his room and board, and it was a debt he would not lightly forget. On the other hand, it was a debt he couldn't begin paying just yet, even though he had the twenty dollars Mr. Weaver gave him for the fight. Arnie needed that money to carry him through until he found Katherine. After that, well, he'd been thinking quite a lot about what to do after they were married. There was work available cutting harness material at Hibbing Leather Works if nothing else. If Katherine thought she could adjust more easily at some distance from her family, then there wasn't any reason why they shouldn't settle right here in Denver. After all, Arnie already had some friends here. And they would love Katherine almost as much as he did. He was sure about that. Once they met her, they would find here as irresistible as he did.

"You'll come back and marry me?" Andy asked, a smile

Frank Roderus

stretching her lips, but her eyes somewhat more serious than a joke like that deserved.

"Don't you think you oughta grow up first?" Arnie said back at her.

"I'm working on it," Andy said seriously. "Give me a couple years. You'll see."

He laughed, a trifle nervously to be sure, and solemnly shook Andy's small hand, then scratched Buttons behind the ears.

And that, as they say, was that. He'd already said his good-byes to Mr. Thomas early that morning, before the fat man left for work.

That one had been really difficult. Arnie owed Mr. Thomas a hell of a lot more than just the dollars that were involved.

"Yeah, well . . ." Arnie'd said awkwardly.

"Take care of yourself, Arnold Rasmussen."

"You too, y'hear?"

Andy looked on the verge of tears, and Arnie would have to admit to having something of a lump in his throat too. Dammit. He shouldered his saddle and bedroll and winked at the girl. "See you later."

"Sure. Later."

It was a long walk to the railroad station, but he had time enough. There wouldn't be an upbound train leaving for Fairplay until afternoon. And he wanted to save the trolley fare. There was no telling how long it might take him to find Katherine in this Mosquito Gulch place, and there were expenses Arnie had to allow for in the meantime.

Even so, it was with a light heart and a spring in his step that Arnie left Mrs. Elroy's boarding house and set out for Fairplay, Colorado, and points beyond.

Chapter Forty-nine

It was shortly before dawn when the narrow-gauge train pulled into the tiny depot, little more than a shack really, a mile or so southeast of Fairplay. According to the conductor's big, bulb-shaped, stem-winding, railroad-certified pocket watch, it was 5:17 A.M. Exactly. And when he stepped down off the steel steps to the cinder-blackened gravel below, Arnie could see his breath. This, he reminded himself, was in the summertime. What it must be like here in winter he did not want to know.

There was a peach-colored tinge on the horizon off toward the east, but not enough light for him to see anything by quite yet.

"This is Fairplay?" he asked of no one in particular. "It sure don't look like much, does it?"

"Town's that way," a passing gentleman in a suit, tie, and bulky coat volunteered, pointing.

"Thanks." Once he knew where to look, he could make out a few pinpoints of light in that direction. Lamps showing in the windows of early-rising folks, he supposed.

There were no hansoms or trolleys here—funny how quick he'd gotten used to the city comforts down in Denver—but there was a fellow who for twenty-five cents would take a passenger and baggage to a hotel, or so he said.

"That sounds a mite high, neighbor."

"It's either that, boy, or walk the mile. Your choice," the driver said rather smugly.

Arnie smiled at him and balanced his tight-rolled rig on one shoulder. "If I don't manage anything else today, then I expect I can earn myself a quarter by walking the distance."

The wagon driver shrugged and gave his attention to other, more agreeable folks. Arnie was halfway to town by the time the wagon rolled past him, sending a cloud of dust into his eyes and making him step lively to get out of the way of the off leader, but otherwise doing no harm.

Fairplay, it turned out, was of a respectable size after all. Arnie just hadn't been able to see that from a distance in the dark. Once he got close, he could see a cluster of low-roofed log houses, a tall hotel building and, just past it, an equally tall stone courthouse.

The downtown business district, he found, lay off to the left a city block. There were lights shining there and some foot traffic despite the hour.

Arnie stopped outside a brightly lighted window and peered inside. The place was a cafe, full of men in rough clothing gathered around the tables like pigs at a trough and every one of them intent on getting some groceries into their bellies before the work day got under way.

It was warm inside the cafe, for which Arnie was grateful. Walking had gotten a little sweat worked up on him, and once he slowed down, the cold had started to give him a chill, so the heat in the cafe was more than welcome.

A man wearing a dirty apron saw him come in and pointed over the heads of the seated crowd to a corner where there was an empty chair. Arnie held his saddle in front of him and maneuvered carefully through the sea of mostly silent men to reach the table. The waiter was there before him. "What will it be, mister?"

"I, uh . . ."

"Menu's on the chalkboard there. Let me know when you make up your mind." Before Arnie had time to respond, the man was gone, sliding between the tables slick as an eel in snot and away into a back room where Arnie presumed the kitchen must be.

The hastily scrawled menu—even Arnie had better hand-writing than that—offered perfectly normal fare. At perfectly outrageous prices. The prices here were way higher even than in Denver, and Denver's prices were enough to make a country boy cringe. Arnie hoped these fellows around him made an awful high wage, because they would surely need it to survive in a hostile environment like this.

The waiter came back, practically slammed a cup of coffee down in front of Arnie, and put his hands on his hips and an impatient look on his face. The man needed a shave, Arnie saw, and a bath wouldn't have hurt any. "Well?"

"The coffee," Arnie said, "and porridge."

"Big spender, huh?" Coffee and oatmeal went for fifteen cents. In Alder Creek he could have gotten the porridge for a nickel with the coffee thrown in free. But then he wasn't in Alder Creek any more.

"No job," Arnie explained.

The waiter looked at him a little more kindly after that. Or anyhow with some degree of sympathy.

Once the waiter left to fetch the oatmeal, Arnie tasted the coffee. There is no such thing as bad coffee, he'd long ago decided. This, however, came close. Still, it was steaming hot and put some warmth into his empty stomach. He hadn't eaten since breakfast the day before at Mrs. Elroy's table. The prices in the railroad dining car had been enough to make this place look cheap, and he simply hadn't been willing to part with that much money for a few lousy bites of food.

"Excuse me," a fellow diner on the far side of the table said.

"Are you talking to me, sir?"

"I am. I believe I heard you say you have no job?"

"That's right, sir."

"We're hiring," the man offered. "Three dollars a day."

Arnie whistled. Three dollars for one single day? Incredible. A top hand didn't make that much. Top hand? Hell, a ranch foreman didn't earn that. Even down in Denver Arnie'd never heard of anybody making that much money. Two dollars a day maybe. And that was for skilled work. Dollar a day was more likely. Up home a regular hand would draw twenty dollars a month and keep. That sure wouldn't go far here. But then what with the prices in this mining town being what they were, he supposed a man would have to make that much just to get along.

"Sound good to you, does it?" the friendly diner observed.

"It would, I guess, except I'm just passing through. On my way to a place called Mosquito Gulch."

"Isn't every-damn-body," the fellow grumbled. "That place is why there's a shortage of manpower in the park now."

"Park, sir? I didn't know there was a park here. Like that federal park up to Yellowstone, you mean?"

The fellow smiled at Arnie's display of ignorance. So did a couple of the other men at the table, but Arnie didn't take offense. Hell, that's why you ask questions, to find out stuff you don't know. Then you don't have to ask again, right?

"Park like in South Park, which is what this basin used to be known as."

"I see. Thank you. You wouldn't happen to know how a man could get himself over to Mosquito Gulch, would you?"

"There's coaches that leave three, four times a day from here."

"Eight dollars each way," another tablemate volunteered. Arnie winced.

"Is it close enough to walk?"

The man who seemed to know something about transportation in the neighborhood said, "That depends on how much time you got, doesn't it? I mean, Kansas City is close enough to walk to if you don't mind the time."

"I was hoping to be there tonight," Arnie said. "Is there a livery where a person can hire a horse?"

"There's a feed dealer down at that end of town," the man said, pointing. "I don't know if Johnny rents out his stock or not, but you can always ask."

Arnie nodded and thanked him. The waiter came back with a huge bowl—it was practically a basin—of sticky, lumpy, steaming hot, and perfectly delicious oatmeal, and Arnie gave his attention to that. Apparently the waiter felt sorry for someone out of work and was trying to be helpful. Which Arnie didn't mind in the least little bit.

He would take his time about getting around this meal, he figured, then go see could he find a horse for hire.

Chapter Fifty

"You're funning me, right?"

"No, sir, I . . ."

"You got to be funning me, boy. Why, this here is a *mining* camp, not some grass patch. Nobody around here messes with saddle horses. Cobs, I got, son. Missouri mules trained to heavy harness. Burros to work down inside the mines. Even a few fancy light horses that'll pull ladies' carriages. But saddle animals? No use for 'em here, so it'd be a waste of feed to keep 'em."

Arnie sighed. Dang it anyway. "In that case, I don't suppose you'd have any idea how a fellow could get to Mosquito Gulch on the cheap?"

"Oh, now, that's another story, ain't it?" the livery man said.

"Is it indeed?"

"You willing to swap a little sweat for your passage, sonny? You look big enough you wouldn't miss it."

"You mean work my way? What is it you need, mister?"

"I sell livestock feed, right? Well, I got a wagon of hay and a trailer of cracked corn to deliver to a man in Mosquito Gulch. I could use some help making up the load. Tell you what. You load my wagon and trailer and ride along to help grease the axles and tend to the stock overnight and like that, and I'll give you free passage alongside of my driver."

"Free passage and keep?" Arnie countered.

The livery man pursed his lips as if in thought. Then he nodded. ''All right, boy. Done.'' He offered his hand to seal the bargain. ''Passage and found.''

''And keep, not found.'' The difference lay between accepting someone else's leftovers and having full meals of his own. Which was not usually much of a difference, but it never hurt to be careful.

''All right, dammit,'' the livery man agreed. ''And keep.''

''Done,'' Arnie said, and accepted the man's shake.

Chapter Fifty-one

Now that it was daylight, Arnie could get a better look at this South Park, where Fairplay was. The man had said it was a basin and so it was, a bowl of rolling grass set amid the mountains. Arnie wasn't sure, but he guessed the size of the basin to be thirty miles or more across from east to west. It was harder to judge how big it might be north to south since from the road to Alma he couldn't see the peaks that would mark the southern fringes.

That might seem strange except that the basin itself was already so high in elevation—it was supposed to be eight, nine thousand feet or so—that it took an almighty tall peak to so much as look like a mountain here. The peaks and knobs to the north and east looked like little more than good-sized hills from where Arnie was. Those to the west, on the other hand, the Mosquito Range, looked darn sure like proper mountains. And if they looked that high when a man was so high up already, then they were damn sure tall. The Mosquitoes provided South Park with one hell of a backdrop.

"We aren't going all the way up on top of those things, are we?" Arnie asked the teamster, a small man with a cast in one eye and a dense black beard that was near as big as the rest of him put together.

"Most about," the freighter said. His name was Leander Winston, and he handled the lines of a ten-mule hitch like he'd been born with leathers in his hands and weaned on a snaffle bit. He drove the long hitch easier than most folks could handle a buggy, and he talked to his mules like they were people. What's more, Arnie would almost have sworn that the mules could understand the things he said to them.

Watching Leander Winston put his hitch together had been an experience, the pocket-sized jehu ambling from one mule to another, stroking and patting and complimenting them extravagantly. And all the while gentling them into place where he wanted them. He baby-talked those mules the way a doting parent will baby-talk a toddler, and one time Winston's praise for an animal got so effusive that Arnie swore he saw the mule blush . . . but maybe smile a bit too.

About the only thing Leander Winston couldn't do was lug heavy articles about. A sack of cracked corn was bigger and heavier than him, or so it looked. But that didn't much matter, because whatever Winston couldn't lift, Arnie could.

Now Arnie's work was done for the time being, and it was time for the driver to begin earning his keep. Arnie lounged on top of the baled hay in the main wagon—the grain was back in the trailer—just behind Winston, while the little fellow took them up the road toward the silver camp of Alma.

"We'll follow the old Leadville road about a third of the way up, then turn south. It's a poor road, but passable." Winston grinned and added, "Mostly." He leaned forward and pointed. "You see that patch of dark color just above the cliffs up there?"

"Uh-huh."

"That's about where the road lies. Once we make the turn we're not but five, six hours from the Gulch."

"Will we make it in tonight?"

"Tomorrow," Winston promised, "God willin' and the creek don't rise."

Arnie knew better than to ask what creek. It was an expression they used up home too. "I was hoping to get there tonight," he said.

"It never hurt anybody to hope for something." The little fellow swiveled his head around and grinned up at his swamper, who was twice his size and half his age. "But we won't see Mosquito Gulch till tomorrow past noon."

"Wake me when we get there," Arnie said, tipping his hat forward and lying back on the sweet-smelling hay.

Chapter Fifty-two

If it had been a matter of sight-seeing that brought him there, then Arnie would have preferred not to see Mosquito Gulch at all. The place was just about the ugliest thing he'd ever laid eyes on.

Set as it was amid the grand, majestic beauty of the tall Colorado mountains—not that they could compare with Wyoming's mountains, of course—Mosquito Gulch had all the appeal of a carbuncle hanging off the nose of a beautiful woman.

The insatiable requirements of the mines had stripped every last speck of wood off the mountainsides for a mile or more in every direction, and that devastation left the land open to the scouring effects of rain and runoff, so that all that was left was gray rock and brown dirt. Arnie had heard about such. It was said the mines delivered gold or silver, but only when fed the wood that was needed to provide shoring, to build shacks, to make steam for the hoists, to cook with . . . whatever. Mines, he'd been told, ran on wood and sweat in roughly equal quantities.

It was one thing to have been told that, of course, and another thing entirely to be confronted with it in person. "Are all mining camps like this?" he asked.

"Of course not," Mr. Winston told him. "Some of them are worse."

"Fairplay doesn't look like this."

Frank Roderus

"Fairplay has been there twenty years or better. There's been time for grass to grow back and wives to plant bushes and stuff. Fairplay used to look this bad or worse."

"Do you mean this valley should be green again in twenty years or so?" Arnie asked, doubt showing plain in his expression.

"Likely," Leander Winston said. "If only because I don't expect Mosquito Gulch to last very long. Most don't, you know. A place booms for a year or two, but unless there's an unusually strong ore body, they mine it all out in no time. Quick as the costs of mining outweigh the income, the mines shut down and everybody moves on to the next big strike." The wagon driver turned and pointed out across the expanse of South Park below them to the east and south. "In those hills out there are the bones of a dozen ghost towns. More'n that probably. In their own time they were all of them just as lively as Mosquito Gulch. Now there's only a few old-timers that can even remember their names."

Arnie could hardly conceive of such an impermanent way. Everything temporary. Nothing anyone could count on, not even the town itself. Stores, churches, whole populations just . . . disappearing and blowing away like smoke on the wind.

Ranching was a matter of building a future. A man saw to the health of his herd and of his grass. He bred his stock and did his best to get by from selling his culls while saving the best as his increase. And in twenty years, thirty, however many it took to fill his land with all the livestock it would carry . . . why then he could maybe afford to buy himself more land and keep right on planning, building, struggling for a better future.

But pick up and go away? Not hardly.

Why, even dirt farmers planted their fields and held back seed with an eye toward permanence and the future.

This uncertain business here? Arnie didn't like the idea of it, never mind the profits that could be taken away when the booms went bust. Arnie wanted to be able to look to something he could count on.

"Not your cup of tea, boy?"

"No, sir, I reckon it's not."

"Mine neither to tell you the truth," Mr. Winston admitted.

176

"I'd rather stick with my teams and let someone else worry about the stuff I haul in and out. What I like is taking my mules down the road. And going home at night to a family that's got food in the larder and a fire on the hearth."

"You got children, Mr. Winston?"

The little man grinned. "Six so far and another one coming." He clucked his tongue and the mules pricked their ears, already leaning forward in their collars in anticipation of the command that was sure to follow. "This last one is sure to be a boy. After six girls in a row, that'll only be fair, right?"

"That sounds right to me," Arnie said agreeably, having no idea at all if it was right or not.

The heavily loaded rig rolled slowly up the rise leading into the narrow gulch that gave the camp its name, the road running parallel to a dark, muddy creek that stank of chemicals and sewage.

"Could I ask you something, Mr. Winston?"

"Of course you can, son."

"Would you happen to know, well, could you tell me, please, which of the bawdy houses here have the prettiest ladies?"

Winston turned and gave him a disapproving look. "I don't know that I'd tell you that, Rasmussen, even if I knew. Didn't I just say I'm a family man?"

"I didn't mean—"

"Not everybody is a rake or a ne'er-do-well, Rasmussen," Winston said primly. "Eighteen years married and I still dote on my wife. Never once cheated on her; never will. You think just because I spend time on the road I have to—"

"Sir. Please. I never meant to imply any such thing. I just—"

"I'd thought better of you than that, boy. You disappoint me."

"Yes, sir. I'm sorry."

They traveled the rest of the way into Mosquito Gulch in a silence that was definitely cool if not downright hostile.

Arnie unloaded the trailer and wagon as quickly as he could, then told Mr. Winston good-bye and took his saddle and bedroll out of the wagon boot. The little man did not see fit to offer a handshake or a word of parting.

Arnie didn't really care all that much, though.

He was in Mosquito Gulch.

And with any kind of luck, any luck at all, he would find Katherine that night and rescue her from the injustice Claude Martin had forced upon her.

His step was light and his hopes high as he shouldered his gear and headed toward the lamplight that was beginning to show along the single street of the town's business district now that an early, east-side-of-the-mountain dusk was falling.

Chapter Fifty-three

Arnie was not at all sure he had the right place. He'd followed the directions the man gave him, but . . . this house looked entirely too respectable to be, well, to be *that* sort of house.

Still, he was sure he'd heard the directions clearly. He let himself in through a gate in the white-painted picket fence—that fence, pale in the moonlight, was the only bright thing he'd seen since first setting foot in this brown and dreary town—and mounted the front stoop.

A pair of small lamps affixed one on either side of the door showed a tasseled bell pull hanging there. Arnie gave it a tug.

Somewhere inside he heard the faint tinkle of the bell, quickly followed by the muted thunder of feet. A good many feet at that. Had he disrupted something, he wondered. Come somehow to the wrong place after all? It was all a puzzlement to him, but he squared his shoulders and swallowed back his uncertainties and resolved to at least wait and see what happened next.

He was conscious of a pair of eyes peering at him from behind an etched glass panel built into the door, and a moment later the latch clicked and the door was pulled open.

A buxom women of forty or more stood there. She was a stout, matronly looking woman in a handsome dress much grander than anything Arnie had ever seen back home. This woman and her gown, he thought, would have fit comfortably in with the fine ladies he'd seen passing in their carriages down in Denver.

Arnie snatched his hat off and held it nervously in both hands. At least he'd had sense enough to leave his saddle and things down in town and hadn't dragged them out here with him. "Pardon me for bothering you, ma'am, but—"

"You got money, boy?"

"Ma'am?"

"Money, I said. You got the wherewithal to come here, kid? You look like you can maybe afford to pay for some half-dollar whore down on crib row. If you want to play here, sonny, the prices start at five bucks and go up to ten. More for all night, but this is a class place, honey. Nobody gets rushed here. Nobody gets robbed. Now show me you have money on you before I say can you come inside."

He expected he'd come to the right house after all, never mind external appearances. "I got money," he said, digging into his pocket for the gold piece Mr. Weaver'd paid him down in Denver.

The stout woman's expression changed when she saw that, and Arnie decided maybe she wouldn't fit into one of those fancy carriages alongside the proper ladies after all. She held her hand out to be paid, but Arnie pretended not to see and tucked the double eagle back into his pocket for safekeeping. He had no intention of paying for some girl's time here and suspected if this woman ever got hold of his money, Arnie would never see it again. "Can I come in?"

The woman swung the door wide open by way of an answer, and he stepped inside.

Now this—the man back in town called it a cathouse—this was what Arnie'd suspected a palace of sin ought to look like.

The furnishings were plush and pretty and the wallpaper a fancy, flocked pattern over top of polished wood wainscoting. The lamp globes were painted all fine and nice with flowers and cherubs and like that, and the paintings on the walls were of scenes with Grecian columns and mostly naked women cavorting with men and satyrs and flute-playing elves.

Mostly, though, what caught his attention—he'd have had to be three days dead for it not to— was the sight of a string of girls standing elbow to elbow in a line, all of them smiling at him and preening and kind of showing their profiles or tossing their curls to catch his eye. It was like each one of them was silently saying, *Take me, mister, take me; see how I smile, mister, see how I smile; I'll make you happy, mister, I surely will.*

Oh, they caught his eye, all right, each and every one of them.

For they weren't wearing a whole lot in the way of clothes.

They had on short silk robes, some of them, the hems of the robes hardly covering more than was necessary, so that their bare legs were exposed for anyone to see.

A couple of them wore outfits so flimsy he could as good as see right through to what was underneath.

There were—he counted—eight girls. Most were plump. All of them were pretty. One girl had a foreign look about her. She had black hair and dark eyes and skin the same shade as good leather. Not that she looked in any way leather-hard, though. She looked soft and . . . well . . .

Arnie coughed. He felt . . . embarrassed. A little bit excited too if the full truth of it be known. There was an unwelcome stirring of response to the sight of so many pretty girls. And to the knowledge that any one of them could be his just for the asking. And of course for the paying. But none of them could ever truly be his. He knew that. These girls were for rent, not for sale, and whatever a man might do with their bodies had nothing to do with their thoughts or their feelings. Arnie understood that just from looking at them.

But oh, Lordy, he did feel the desire rise within him just the same. They were so *pretty*. And so available.

"Well?" the madam demanded. "Are you gonna pick a girl or not?"

"I, um . . ."

"Yes or no, boy? Five dollars, take your pick."

"I . . . you said you have ten-dollar girls too?" Katherine was not among these whores. Thank God.

"I got two girls worth that much. One of them's available right now. You want to see that one?"

"Yes, ma'am, please."

"He don't want to pick none of you just yet," the woman announced.

Almost before Arnie knew what was happening, there was a faint rustle of cloth, and the lineup of girls disappeared, the whole bunch of them scattering like a covey of quail and fading away into other, unseen rooms. Apparently these girls did not display their charms unless there was the possibility of a reward to come from it.

"Set over there, boy. I'll fetch Althea and you can see does she suit you better."

"Yes, ma'am, thank you."

The madam was gone for only a minute. Following on her heels when she returned was a pale, chestnut-haired girl who had sunken cheekbones, arms hardly bigger around than pipe stems, a hairstyle that must have taken hours to construct, and a low-cut gown that would have graced any high society ball. The girl looked like she could not have been more than fifteen, sixteen years old, and there was a look about her—something in her huge, washed-out gray eyes—that reminded Arnie of the stricken look he'd seen once on a neck-shot fawn that couldn't move to get away but knew a knife was fixing to cut its throat there where it lay.

"Althea will please you, kid, I promise. Two full hours for ten dollars, and she'll do anything you want for that time."

"Yes, ma'am. I think . . . you said you have another girl here?"

"That one's not available. I also told you that."

"Will she be? Later, I mean?"

"Maybe. Maybe not."

"I'd like to see her before I decide on a girl," Arnie said. "You understand, don't you? I mean, this is the biggest, most important thing I've ever done in my whole life and—"

"Are you telling me you're a damn virgin, kid?" the woman said loudly. Arnie winced. Why, anyone might overhear. Who knows what all they might think.

He didn't answer. Not in so many words. But he surely did blush, the heat rushing into his cheeks so hot he felt he would warm the whole damn house and never have need of a stove.

"Did you come here to bust your cherry? Lord love you,

son, why didn't you say so? You wait right there. Take your time. Just let me know when you make up your mind what girl you want. An' when you do, kid, I'll whisper in her ear, hear? Make sure she's extra gentle with you.''

The old bawd reached down to take a fold of Arnie's cheek between her thumb and forefinger. She gave him a mildly painful pinch, then patted his knee. "Don't you worry, lad. You'll leave this house happy.''

"Yes, ma'am, thank you.''

Chapter Fifty-four

The longer he sat there the better Arnie understood why the madam hadn't wanted to let him in right off. He felt awkward and out of place, every inch the country bumpkin he supposed he really was.

It was the upper crust of Mosquito Gulch that came boldly in or slipped surreptitiously out afterward. The gentlemen wore suits and ties and fine vests, or the high-topped lace-up boots that proclaimed they were engineers and surveyors and like that.

Regardless of what else they looked like, these gentlemen looked like quality. Educated folk with proper manners and breeding and money to spend.

No, this was definitely not Arnie's element. Still, he wouldn't have left if he'd been paid to. He had to wait until he had seen every last girl who worked there.

Not that he really expected to find Katherine there. Not once he realized that in a place like this there were no bar hustlers trying to convince the gents to spend on whiskey or wine. All the girls here save the madam were whores, and probably even the madam was a former whore herself. No, he really didn't expect to find Katherine there. But he did not want to leave until he was sure.

And after his experiences down in Denver, he did not think it wise to come right out and ask about a red-haired lass named

Katherine. Or Irish Kate as she'd called herself when she was at Mr. Weaver's place.

Just in case.

So Arnie sat and observed and smiled at whoever came near.

He got himself something of an education, by gum.

Whoever came calling would give a yank on the bell pull, and the silver bell mounted inside the door would ring out its merry call and that was the signal for all the girls who were not otherwise occupied to come rushing into the parlor and form into a line.

The madam spent most of her time in the foyer or elsewhere, but she never opened the door until the girls were formed up and ready. Then she would take a peek outside before opening up.

Twice while Arnie sat there she refused entry to men—common working men, he supposed, or those without funds enough to make their entry worth her while—and once she got into a brief, overloud argument with a peddler who was reluctant to take no for an answer.

That brought out a squat, heavily muscled bouncer from somewhere in the back of the house. The man was bald as a cue ball, making up for that deficit with a ferocious mustache and a scowl fit to wilt steel bars. One look at the bouncer and the peddler's recalcitrance melted clean away and the man left without a whimper. Arnie didn't blame him. Even if Mr. Thomas had been there to lend assistance, Arnie would not have wanted to face anyone that strong and mean-looking across the floor of a boxing ring.

Once Arnie was approached by a blond young lady with blue eyes, rouge-smeared cheeks, and bosoms that would have put a dairy cow to shame. When she sat down beside him, he found his gaze drifting south to dwell in the powdered valley between her bosoms. It was rude, he knew, but he couldn't help himself. There was so much of it to see there. And dang near all of it on display. Arnie found himself becoming a trifle overwarm, and shifted uncomfortably from side to side. The girl didn't seem to mind.

"Mrs. Baxter told us this is your first time, honey. I want

185

you to know, if you pick me, I'll teach you things you won't ever forget. You know?'' She reached out and laid a hand on his knee. Arnie could feel the heat of her flesh clean through the cloth of his trousers. It unnerved him. But he could not honestly say that he didn't like it either.

''I, um, thank you, miss.''

The blond girl smiled sweetly. Then she reached farther up his leg—all the way up his leg, actually—and touched him. She actually touched him. Right there. Britches and all.

Her smile never changed. Not a lick.

Arnie thought sure he was going to die of embarrassment. Or from something, he wasn't sure what.

Heat rushed into his cheeks again and must have showed up plain, because the girl laughed, and so did the dark-haired girl who had come into the room again, and another, plainer girl with mouse-brown hair. Oh, they were all getting a kick out of his discomfort now.

''Don't be a tease, Wanda. It isn't ladylike.''

''Yes'm, Mrs. Baxter,'' Wanda said with syrupy false contriteness.

The madam looked like she was going to say more, but just then another girl came up behind her and tugged on the sleeve of her gown. Mrs. Baxter leaned down a bit so the message could be delivered in a whisper into her ear. Then she straightened. ''Are you sure?''

''That's what Linda told me to tell you, ma'am.''

The madam's expression hardened and became cold. ''Get James for me, child. Right now. And you, all of you''—she motioned to the girls in the parlor—''out. Right now.''

There wasn't any lollygagging. The girls obeyed as quickly and as unquestioningly as a clutch of well-trained sheepdogs, wheeling about and trotting briskly out of sight to wherever they spent their time between bell rings.

Mrs. Baxter for some reason gave Arnie a withering glare, then she too turned and stormed away.

He suspected there was trouble with one of the customers, and probably at this moment she was disgusted with men in general, for certainly he had done nothing to provoke her.

He settled back on the sofa where he'd been perched for so

long, wondering if he would find Katherine tonight after all, for the hour was growing late and there were still at least two cheaper cathouses and a whole host of saloons to visit before he could be sure if Katherine had come here when she left Denver.

Arnie yawned and decided he soon would have to give some thought to where he would sleep tonight. It had been a long day and wasn't over with yet.

Chapter Fifty-five

The James that Mrs. Baxter referred to turned out to be the bald, burly bouncer Arnie had seen earlier. And it wasn't some rowdy customer the man intended to throw out of the place. It was Arnie.

"You!" the bouncer snapped when he came into the parlor. Arnie stood, wanting to ask what the problem was. Before he could open his mouth to form the question, James threw his first punch.

Arnie blocked it without taking time for conscious thought. The training Mr. Thomas had given to him came into play, and Arnie flicked the punch aside with a quick swipe of his left forearm. "Hey, listen, what've I—?"

James tried again, this time with a left. Arnie met it with his other forearm and deflected it wide. The blow would likely have taken his head off had it landed. But it did not.

"Listen, dammit, what is this?"

James threw a short, sharp underhand blow that was supposed to land in Arnie's belly and double him over. Arnie stepped quickly to his left, pulling James out of position. Arnie could have hurt the man then with a left hook to the kidney, but he still couldn't quite believe that a scrap was inevitable. If he could just get the man to *listen*. . . .

"Get him, James," Mrs. Baxter hissed from the other side of the room. "Hurt him before you throw him out. Hurt him bad."

Hayseed

It began to occur to Arnie that no one here was particularly interested in listening to anything that he wanted to say. His side of the story—whatever story this was—just wasn't welcome.

James spun to face him and, head bobbing and hands extended more like he wanted to wrestle than to box, began to stalk Arnie across the heavy, floral-print rug that softened the floor and deadened the sound of his footsteps so that all Arnie could hear at the moment—all he was listening to, anyway—was the muted whistle of James's heavy breathing as the bouncer tried to trap him in a corner.

That was almost funny, Arnie thought. Hell, Arnie'd spent practically his whole life sitting on top of good horses trained to cut calves out of herds and make the stubborn bovines go where they were wanted in spite of their own natural instincts. And putting a man into a corner and keeping him there was just another form of cutting cows, except probably easier. After all, folks weren't half as wild as those spooky old range cattle, and Arnie could handle them easy enough.

He could see two steps before James took them where the man wanted to go and how he expected to get there. Arnie let him think it was all working just nice as you please. Then, about the time James thought he had himself a calf trapped tight into a corner, Arnie quit pretending and let James know that he wasn't facing some city boy here. Arnie feinted ducking to his left, stopped the motion, and stood tall while he hammered James's face with a hard, straight right.

Damn punch stung Arnie about as bad as it must have hurt James, and Arnie wondered if he could call a time-out so he could find his gloves and pull them on. Somehow he didn't much think James would go for that.

The bouncer blinked, but he didn't yet look like he realized there was anything different about this latest in his string of victims. He shook his head, spraying some blood that was beginning to stream out of a broken nose, and once again crouched as he bulled his way straight ahead.

Obviously the man expected Arnie to back away. Instead, Arnie moved close. Quickly. And sent a crushing blow into James's breadbasket. James turned pale and the wind was forced out of him in a great, wheezing whoosh.

While James was preoccupied with trying to regain his breath, Arnie stepped lightly to his left and tattooed the bouncer's eyebrows and forehead with a rapid-fire series of left jabs. The combination didn't do a hell of a lot of good for Arnie's knuckles, but it did have the desired result. James commenced bleeding from fresh cuts over his eyes as well as from his already busted nose.

If this kept up much longer, Arnie thought, the inside of this parlor was going to look more like an abattoir than a fine and fancy whorehouse.

James still hadn't quite caught up with the notion of what was going on here. And Arnie had no intention of letting him make any adjustments either, for, as powerful as the man looked to be, Arnie thought it best that he not find himself on the receiving end of too many of the punches that were flying between them.

James punched. Arnie weaved and bobbed and ducked.

James punched. Arnie flicked his wrists, deflecting James's fists, and responded with hard countering punches of his own.

James punched. Arnie danced lightly backward until James ducked his head and plodded forward, only to be met by sudden assaults that left his ears stinging and his eyes full of his own blood.

James punched and Arnie steeled himself to accept some damage to his own hands. He wanted to end this. Soon, before the bouncer tagged him with a lucky shot. He began concentrating on the shelf of the burly fellow's jaw, hoping to drop him and put him out of the game with a carefully placed right that he would throw with all his weight and leg strength behind it.

"Get him, you son of a bitch," the madam was screaming at her employee. "Don't let that kid do this to you."

James stopped still. He was in the center of the parlor, blood dripping off his chin and his elbows onto the rug. His head was hanging, and after that short flurry he looked exhausted, used up and worn out. It was obvious he wasn't accustomed to anyone standing up to him. He especially was not used to the idea that anyone who did stand up to him could do so with impunity, the punishment going James's way and not that of the unwelcome customer. James eyed Arnie like a played-out bull while with slow and deliberate care he reached into a back pocket for a soiled bandanna. He shook it out and then used its folds to clear the blood from his eyes.

"Can we talk about this?" Arnie asked. "Will you at least tell me what's wrong? Why you're doing this?"

James didn't answer him and neither did Mrs. Baxter. She was still much too busy shouting threats and curses to pay attention to anyone else. Arnie wasn't sure if her fury was directed more toward him or toward the ineffective bouncer who hadn't been able to beat up on what had looked like easy pickings. Not that he supposed it really mattered overmuch.

James finished wiping his face, stood, and gulped deep for some air.

"Are you done, mister?"

James didn't answer. He looked at the blood-soaked kerchief, then shrugged and carefully folded it before returning it to his back pocket.

But this time, when his hand came forward again, Arnie could see the glint of steel in it.

The man had a knife. And he held it like he knew how to use the ugly, scary thing. He held it low, cutting edge upward and the butt of the haft nestled in his palm. Arnie knew absolutely nothing about knives or how to fight with them—that hadn't been any part of Mr. Thomas's course of instruction—but he knew enough to be scared half out of his wits by the sight of the deadly looking blade.

This fight was turning into something a hell of a lot more serious than anything he'd ever experienced before. This fight was not just for fun, not for bragging rights, not even for domination. This fight could be to the death if the bouncer and the screeching madam had their way.

Arnie backed away slowly, feeling behind him with his feet before committing his weight, eyes never leaving James. More accurately, with his eyes never leaving the slowly weaving point of James's knife. The blade had an almost hypnotic effect on Arnie. His mouth had gone dry, and his breath was coming short and shallow.

There was nowhere behind him to run. James stood between Arnie and the wide double doorway into the foyer. Mrs. Baxter and a dimly perceived bunch of female faces filled the smaller doorframe that led into the back of the house. Arnie was trapped, pure and simple. He figured he knew now what a calf felt like when it faced a good cutting horse. Except the fate of the calf wasn't likely to be half as bad as what James seemed to have planned for Arnie.

Lordy, Arnie thought, the single, silent word as much a prayer for delivery as it was an exclamation of despair.

He backed up hard against an end table beside the sofa where he'd sat earlier. James took a step toward him. Then another. The knife caught a shaft of bright lamplight and reflected it off the walls and the ceiling.

James came forward another step.

Arnie reached behind him, his hand fumbling for . . . something, anything, he didn't know what, didn't care. Anything.

The only thing on the table was the coal oil lamp, its hand-painted globe hot and bright, its base heavy with lightly scented oil.

If that was all there was then that would have to do, wouldn't it?

Arnie picked up the lamp. Threw the thing. If it started a fire . . . hell, if it started a fire, so what? This wasn't his place, and he didn't have any reason to care about Mrs. Baxter's future well-being, did he? Not when certain questions about Arnie's own future had yet to be determined.

He threw the lamp as hard as he could, straight at the knife in James's hand.

The brittle globe shattered, and the weight of the much heavier glass base knocked the knife from James's grasp. The flame blew out once the protection of the globe was gone, thank goodness, and what was left of the lamp scattered harmlessly over the rug. Nobody had better walk barefoot in there until the dang rug was taken out and thoroughly beaten. But then it would need some cleaning to get James's blood out of it anyway, wouldn't it?

"Kill him!" Mrs. Baxter shouted from the doorway. "Kill the SOB!"

James didn't so much as look to see where his knife had fallen. He reached behind him, on the other side this time, to dip into a different back pocket.

And this time what he produced was even scarier than the knife had been.

This time he had a pistol in his hand. A revolver. Small. A shiny, nickel-plated thing.

The weapon's small size did nothing to make it less awful.

Arnie looked into the muzzle of the little gun. It seemed to be aimed, he thought, pretty much at the bridge of his nose. He could see the dull gray tips of bullets at the front of the open chambers of the cylinder.

He could see James's broad, blood-smeared finger on the trigger.

He could see James's finger begin to move.

Oh God, Arnie thought. This was not the way things were supposed to've been.

Chapter Fifty-six

"No! Don't."

A pale shape with some white, billowy stuff floating behind it came barreling through the mob of onlookers in the doorway and sprang forward to throw itself between James and Arnie.

"Don't kill him, for God's sake. You don't have to kill him."

It wasn't a ghost in front of him, Arnie saw now, but a woman. One of the whores, he supposed. She was wearing a flimsy nightgown sort of thing the like of which he'd noticed—paid especial attention to, in fact—in some of those mail order catalog things but never ever expected to see for real, and in particular never expected to see with a human female person inside of it. If he hadn't still been so scared of James and that pistol, Arnie likely would have been more embarrassed than he was. And even in spite of that rather powerful distraction, he couldn't help but notice that the garment—it hardly deserved to be called a garment—hid practically nothing from him.

The woman wearing it was big, with a shapely figure and unnaturally red hair. Her back was to him as she pleaded with first James and then Mrs. Baxter to spare Arnie.

"I'll take care of this. I promise. He won't be a bother again. I'll . . . I'll get him to leave. I'll talk to him. He won't come back."

194

Mrs. Baxter hesitated. Then she shrugged. "This was your idea to begin with, dearie."

"Not . . . I can't let you kill him. Not that. Please."

"It doesn't matter one way or the other to me, honey. I told you I'd protect you, and that is what we're trying to do now."

"Yes, ma'am, I know that, thank you. But I can't let you kill him."

Mrs. Baxter made a sour face and looked at the damage that had been done to her parlor.

"I'll take care of everything. I promise I will."

"James, put the gun away," the madam ordered.

James looked like he didn't much care for the instruction, but he obeyed it without comment. The pistol disappeared, and he located his knife, picked it up, and tucked that out of sight also. Arnie breathed a little easier once James did that. And a whole lot more easily still when the bouncer said something too softly for Arnie to overhear and then pushed his way through the crowd of painted girls who still clogged the doorway.

"All right, ladies. The show's over. You can go back to your rooms now."

The silver bell rang, and all the girls hurried to form a line across the bloody, glass-strewn rug while Mrs. Baxter gave them a moment to get into place and then made for the front door.

The tall whore with the bottle-red hair took Arnie by the hand and led him away into a hallway and on to a warm kitchen that smelled of naphtha soap and fresh-baked bread. The smells made Arnie homesick.

"Damn you!" the whore snapped, wheeling to face him.

Chapter Fifty-seven

It took Arnie several long, disbelieving seconds to make himself believe that it was his own sweet Katherine underneath all that rouge and paint and powder. She had globs of dark, sticky-looking stuff smeared around her eyes and blue gunk on the eyelids and red stuff on her lips and more red stuff overlying the powder on her cheeks, and she looked like a damned circus clown more than the girl Arnie knew and as good as grew up with in Alder Creek, Wyoming.

"Katherine? I can't . . . what have they done to you? How did you . . . ?" He shook his head. "Never mind. You don't have to tell me anything. And I'll never ask again. I promise. I . . . I came to rescue you, Katherine. I came to take you home if you'll come back with me. If not . . . I've thought this out real careful since that man Martingale—did you know his real name is Claude Martin and he's married?—since he went and kidnapped you, and if you don't want to go back where everybody knows what happened, then we'll get married—I've already looked into that and we can do it down in Denver, at the courthouse, I've even asked a good friend of mine there to stand up with us and I know a girl who'd be our second witness; there have to be two, you understand—and I can get a job there, in fact I've already found one, and we can stay at Mrs. Elroy's boarding house to start, just until we can afford a place of our own, and either way we'll let your folks and

196

mine know that we're both safe and that everything is fine, and—''

"Arnie."

He tried to say some more, but Katherine stepped forward and put a hand to his lips to shush him. Her hand felt hot and dry, and he suspected she was coming down sick with something and he told her that and said, "You don't have to worry about anything now, Katherine. I'll take care of you. Whatever happens, I'll take care of you. I'll take good care of you for always, and—''

"Arnie, shut up."

"But—''

"Shut up, Arnie."

One of the girls came into the kitchen, but Katherine sent her packing with a coldly hostile look that was more than rebuke enough. "Come along outside, Arnie. I don't want any of the other girls to listen in. You don't know what they're like." She sniffed. "Jealous bitches."

"Katherine honey, you shouldn't ought to use language like that. People will think—''

"I told you to shut up, Arnie. I meant it. And people here know that I'm a whore. I don't think a little crude language is going to shock anyone."

"But that's the thing, honey, you don't have to . . . that is to say, you aren't really a . . . one of those. Like those other girls, I mean. Sweetheart, you're—''

Katherine spun around, her hand coming up before he had a chance to see what she was about. Her palm cracked across his cheek with a sound like a gunshot, the force of the slap enough to turn his jaw and make his cheek sting like hell.

"Honey?"

Katherine's eyes turned cold and as hard as her clothing and ugly makeup made her out to look. She fairly hissed when she said, "Don't you never, *ever* call me that. D'you hear me, Arnold Rasmussen? Don't you ever call me honey. Nor dear. Nor sweetie. Nor any of those sappy, stupid pet names. I hear them all damn night every damn night, stupid smelly men pawing at my tits and slobbering over my cheek and making believe I'm their honey-pie. I hate it. I hate them. I hate you

197

most of all, damn you. So don't you ever again call me by one of those dumb names or I'll . . . I'll . . . I'll cut your nuts off. I swear I will."

"But . . . Katherine?"

"Jesus, Arnie, you look like a gutshot deer or something. Strap your chin up so it isn't hanging down at your knees and listen to me. Chance—Claude if you like—he didn't kidnap anybody. I begged him to take me with him. I told him what all I'd do to pay him for his trouble, and believe me, that was one happy son of a bitch for the little while we were together. Then I told him to go back to his wife and leave me alone, because if I ever saw him again I'd do to him the same as I just promised you. Chance, he had sense enough to believe that I'd do it. And he was right. I only hope you're that smart too, because I wasn't lying to you, Arnie. The only reason I'm out here talking and freezing my damn butt off is so maybe you'll smarten up and leave me the hell alone. Do you hear me? I had a good thing going down at Weaver's, but you had to come around and screw that up for me. Well I'm not going to let you do the same here. Do you know how much money I make, Arnie? For something I used to do anyway just for the fun of it? Chance didn't get a virgin when he carried me off, Arnie. Did you know that? Didn't you ever hear any of the boys bragging? Sure they did. I slept with half the boys in town. I liked it. Always did, and so did they. So Chance wasn't getting anything close to a virgin when he got me. Of course, the fun is gone now, but it isn't all that big a loss. The thing is, Arnie, I like what I'm doing now. I like having money and being able to smoke and drink and do whatever I damn please. I'm not some soiled dove who's been forced into the sporting life. I'm a whore, Arnie. I'm a whore because I *like* being a whore. I like sleeping till afternoon and being waited on by a maid. You think I'd ever have a maid back in stupid Alder Creek? We both know better. Back there I'd be old and wrinkled before my time. We both know that too."

Arnie looked at her, at the powder caked thick in the creases of her neck and the pores of what he'd always thought of as a perfect complexion and . . . God, Katherine had been a whore for just a matter of weeks now, and already she looked like she was thirty, maybe thirty-five years old. She was seventeen, for God's sake. She wouldn't turn eighteen until August. Arnie remembered that for certain sure, for he'd been one of the young people at the church who attended her sixteenth birthday party less than two years back. And now . . . Jesus! Old and wrinkled before her time? He guessed so.

"I still—"

"Go home, Arnie. Tell my folks you couldn't find me. But tell them . . . I don't know. Think up something. Tell them Chance and me got married and you think we're still in Denver, but you couldn't find me. You say Martingale isn't the SOB's real name? That's perfect. If they ever try and find him, us, under that name, it won't be possible. They can go right on thinking that everything is all right but that I'm too ashamed to write and tell them how things are. Will you do that for me, Arnie?"

"But what about . . . I told you I'd marry you, Katherine. No one would ever have to know about . . . any of this."

"Arnie, you're sweet, but sometimes, I swear, you're God-awful stupid too. If you were to marry me, Arnie, I'd be cheating on you in less than a week, and run away from you with the first slick-haired son of a bitch that'd take me along. It would be Chance Martingale all over again, except this time it would be you I was running from and not my folks and the boring life in Alder Creek. Don't you understand that, Arnie? Can't you see what I'm telling you?"

"But I thought . . . I mean . . ." He could feel moist heat swelling behind his eyes and making it difficult for him to see. "I thought . . ."

"Go home, Arnie. You'll find a girl someday. She'll want all those same dull things you do, and she'll be a good wife to you. Scrub your damn clothes and birth your sons, daughters too if you're unlucky, and when you die from old age and overwork, she'll be there to wash you and dress you and put you in the ground. But that girl won't be me, Arnie. Never could have been me. You've always been too blind to see what I really am. Well look. Right now. Look good, Arnie. This is the real me."

She ripped at the neck of her gown and the flimsy cloth

199

parted, falling back to show Katherine's nakedness. Rouged in some places. Purpled with dark bruises in others. Naked. Used. That was mostly it. In her nakedness she looked used much more than she looked alluring or desirable.

Arnie gasped and quickly turned his eyes away. This was something he didn't . . . "Please. Don't."

"Don't follow me no more, Arnie. Go home. Don't come back here, or next time I'll let James do whatever he pleases, and if he doesn't do you hurt, I will. I'll slice 'em right off, Arnie, I swear it."

He felt a faint puff of wind and sensed more than saw that Katherine was passing by him. There was the same impression of pale, billowing cloth that he'd had before. And then the slamming of a door. It felt like the door had closed hard and tight on his heart. He could feel it clamped on him there like a vice.

Jesus!

Blindly he stumbled off the back stoop of Mrs. Baxter's whorehouse. Blindly he made his way back to the saloon where he'd left his saddle and bedroll.

Blind. He'd been blind for years, he supposed.

He kind of wished he still was.

Chapter Fifty-eight

The second set of good-byes was easier than the first had been. He'd worked for ten weeks at Hibbing Leather Works, saving every penny he could, to pay Mr. Thomas back what they both thought was a reasonable amount.

In all that time, Arnie hadn't ever once mentioned what he'd found when he got to the mountains. Nor did anyone ask him what happened there. He supposed they knew. Sort of. The nice thing was that they didn't pry for details.

"You're sure you have enough food to last?" Andrea asked him for probably the tenth time that same morning.

"If your mama's basket got any heavier, I'd have to hire somebody to help me carry it. Then I'd have to feed my helper too, and that would kinda defeat the purpose, wouldn't it?"

"You have your train ticket?" Mr. Thomas asked, for probably the tenth time that same morning. He seemed as worried about Arnie losing his ticket as Andy did that he wouldn't have enough to eat.

Arnie produced the ticket from an inside pocket and showed it to Mr. Thomas, since that seemed about the only way to satisfy the man. "I'll reach Cheyenne before nightfall. Isn't that amazing? All that way and I'll be there in time for supper."

"You'll be careful, won't you?" Andy asked him.

"I'll be careful," he assured her.

"And you'll write to me. You promised you'd write to me. Lots and lots."

"I already promised. Every letter you write to me, kid, I'll answer with one back at you."

The girl laughed and practically wriggled with delight.

"I think you've let yourself in for something, son," Mr. Thomas said. "I think Andy has something in mind for you."

Arnie blushed. And refused to rise to that fat bait. Why, Andy wasn't but a kid. Now. He cocked his head and gave the kid a closer look. Naw! Couldn't ever happen. That is, she was cute. Kind of. But she was just a kid. Now. He caught where these thoughts seemed to be taking him and blushed again.

"Remember," she prompted him. "You promised."

"I won't forget." And he wouldn't either. He would write. As often as she wrote to him, he would. He'd said it, and he would keep his word.

"You have enough cash to buy your stuff back in Cheyenne?" Mr. Thomas asked.

"Enough for my horse if the man don't try to cheat me. Or some other if he's been sold off already. I guess . . . I guess that doesn't matter as much as I used to think it would."

"You've grown up since you got here, son. You know that, don't you?"

"Have I?" Arnie himself was not so sure of that. After all, growing up meant that stuff no longer hurt so bad. Grown men could take it. They were immune from hurts of the heart and stupid stuff like that. Weren't they?

He picked up his saddle and the food basket Mrs. Elroy had packed for him and headed in the direction of the trolley that would carry him out to the train depot and the way home.

Was he really grown now, like Mr. Thomas said? Was this all there was to it?

Arnie wished he knew the answer to that. If he knew that, well, maybe then he'd feel grown. As it was, though, he still had hurts and doubts and uncertainties.

He did know one thing for sure, though. He was going home. For now he supposed that was answer enough.

BRANDISH

DOUGLAS HIRT

FIRST TIME IN PAPERBACK!

Captain Ethan Brandish has finally given up his command of Fort Lowell, deep in Apache territory. But the vicious Apache leader, Yellow Shirt, has another fate in store for him. He and a group of renegade warriors attack a stage station and ride off just before Brandish arrives. But the Apaches are still out there—watching and waiting—and Brandish must risk his own life to save the few wounded survivors.

___4323-8 $4.50 US/$5.50 CAN

Dorchester Publishing Co., Inc.
P.O. Box 6640
Wayne, PA 19087-8640

Please add $1.75 for shipping and handling for the first book and $.50 for each book thereafter. NY, NYC, and PA residents, please add appropriate sales tax. No cash, stamps, or C.O.D.s. All orders shipped within 6 weeks via postal service book rate. Canadian orders require $2.00 extra postage and must be paid in U.S. dollars through a U.S. banking facility.

Name_____

Address_____

City_____ State_____ Zip_____

I have enclosed $_____ in payment for the checked book(s).

Payment <u>must</u> accompany all orders. ☐ Please send a free catalog.

BREAK THE YOUNG LAND

T. V. OLSEN

Winner of the Golden Spur Award

Borg Vikstrom and his fellow Norwegian farmers are captivated when they see freedom's beacon shining from the untamed prairies near a Kansas town called Liberty. In order to stake their claim for the American dream they will risk their lives and cross an angry ocean. But in the cattle barons' kingdom, sodbusters seldom get a second chance...before being plowed under. With a power-hungry politico ready to ignite a bloody range-war, it is all the stalwart emigrant can do to keep the peace...and dodge the price that has been tacked on his head.

_4226-6 $4.50 US/$5.50 CAN

RIP-ROARIN' ACTION AND ADVENTURE BY THE WORLD'S MOST CELEBRATED WESTERN WRITER!

GUN GENTLEMEN

MAX BRAND

Renowned throughout the Old West, Lucky Bill has the reputation of a natural battler. Yet he is no remorseless killer. He only outdraws any gunslinger crazy enough to pull a six-shooter first. Then Bill finds himself on the wrong side of the law, and plenty of greenhorns and gringos set their sights on collecting the price on his head. But Bill refuses to turn tail and run. He swears he'll clear his name and live a free man before he'll be hunted down and trapped like an animal.

_3937-0 $4.50 US/$5.50 CAN

BACK TO MALACHI

ROBERT J. CONLEY
THREE-TIME SPUR
AWARD-WINNER

Charlie Black is a young half-breed caught between two worlds. He is drawn to the promise of the white man's wealth, but torn by his proud heritage as a Cherokee. Charlie's pretty young fiancée yearns for the respectability of a Christian marriage and baptized children. But Charlie can't forsake his two childhood friends, Mose and Henry Pathkiller, who live in the hills with an old full-blooded Indian named Malachi. When Mose runs afoul of the law, Charlie has to choose between the ways of his fiancée and those of his friends and forefathers. He has to choose between surrender and bloodshed.

___4277-0 $3.99 US/$4.99 CAN